‘Why did
asked softl

‘Back?’

‘To my apartme

He hesitated. ‘I forgot something.’

‘What?’

Surrendering to the inevitable, he gave a weary sigh, tired of fighting, and took the small stride that put her in reach. ‘This,’ he murmured, and, lifting his hands, he cupped her face oh, so gently, and lowered his mouth to hers.

Caroline Anderson has the mind of a butterfly. She's been a nurse, a secretary, a teacher, run her own soft-furnishing business and now she's settled on writing. She says, 'I was looking for that elusive something. I finally realised it was variety, and now I have it in abundance. Every book brings new horizons and new friends, and in between books I have learned to be a juggler. My teacher husband John and I have two beautiful and talented daughters, Sarah and Hannah, umpteen pets and several acres of Suffolk that nature tries to reclaim every time we turn our backs!' Caroline also writes for the Mills & Boon® Tender Romance™ series.

Recent titles by the same author:

THE BABY FROM NOWHERE
(Medical Romance™)
ASSIGNMENT: CHRISTMAS
(Medical Romance™)
THE PREGNANT TYCOON
(Tender Romance™)
HOLDING OUT FOR A HERO
(Medical Romance™)
A BRIDE WORTH WAITING FOR
(Tender Romance™)

MATERNAL INSTINCT

BY

CAROLINE ANDERSON

MILLS & BOON®

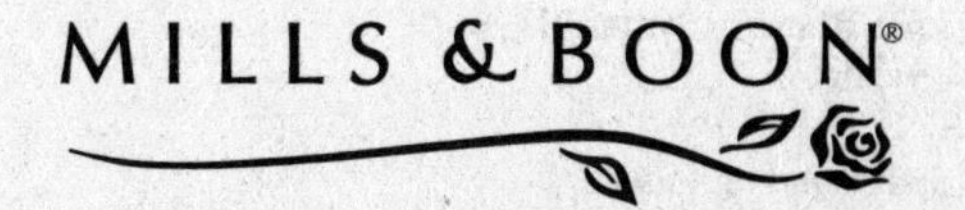

All the characters in this book have no existence outside the imagination of the author, and have no relation whatsoever to anyone bearing the same name or names. They are not even distantly inspired by any individual known or unknown to the author, and all the incidents are pure invention.

First published in Great Britain 2006
Harlequin Mills & Boon Limited,
Eton House, 18-24 Paradise Road, Richmond, Surrey TW9 1SR

Standard ISBN 0 263 84734 9
Promotional ISBN 0 263 85095 1

Set in Times Roman 10½ on 11½ pt.
03-0606-49583

Printed and bound in Spain
by Litografia Rosés, S.A., Barcelona

CHAPTER ONE

HE KNEW who she was straight away.

The formal suit, the neat court shoes—they stood out a mile among the relatives in their casual clothes and the hospital staff in their scrubs and tunics and white coats. If that wasn't enough, the set of her shoulders and the distracted way she was staring out of the landing window while her teeth raked that soft, full lower lip were dead giveaways.

She was a nice-looking girl, he thought irrelevantly. Pretty.

Well, no, probably not pretty in the conventional sense, because her nose was a little crooked and her chin a little too firm, at least from that angle, but she was certainly interesting. She interested Hugh, anyway, and as he climbed the last three stairs he was able to study her for a moment, undetected.

Mmm. Very interesting. Slender, elegant—and not nearly as composed as she would have liked to be, he'd bet his life.

He ought to walk past her, say 'Good morning' politely and go and start the process, but for some reason he paused, fascinated by the way she caught the side of her bottom lip in her teeth again and worried it gently as she stared into the distance.

'Interview?' he murmured, even though he knew the answer.

His voice startled her, and she looked towards him, her eyes scanning the area as if to check that he really was talking to her. Those soft grey eyes, thoughtful and wary, flicked over his suit and back to his face, checking him out. 'Yes. You, too?'

He nodded slowly. Well, it wasn't really a lie…

'A fellow victim,' she said with a rueful grin, before honesty could raise its head. 'I'm Eve Spicer.'

She held out her hand, and he took it. It was slim and cool, her handshake firm despite the slight tremor he could feel in her arm.

For some reason he didn't want to examine, he withheld his name, just smiled and held her hand slightly longer than was strictly necessary before releasing it, dragging out the subterfuge a moment longer. 'Good to meet you, Eve,' he said.

Her pretty mouth twisted wryly, that bottom lip a little pinker where she'd nibbled it. 'I wish I could say it was mutual, but if we're after the same job I think I'm screwed.'

He felt his brows twitch together at her refreshing honesty, and guilt tugged harder at him but, instead of coming clean, he found himself asking, 'Why?'

Her smile became rueful. 'Because I've lost the last two jobs to a man. It might be coincidence but, whatever, it's beginning to be a habit.'

'Habits can be broken. Perhaps it'll be third time lucky.'

She gave a little shrug, frustration showing in the line of her shoulders. 'Maybe. I'm beginning to wonder if I'm doing something wrong in my interviews. Perhaps it won't matter so much for a temporary post—or am I deluding myself? Seem to do a lot of that these days, but I really want this job, even though it's only covering sick leave, because I know someone who was his SHO last year, and she said Hugh Douglas is wonderful to work with and a brilliant teacher. She learnt so much from him.'

Wonderful? Brilliant? He squashed his ego back into its box and wondered to whom he owed this amazing PR. Probably Kate. He'd have to thank her. 'I'm sure you can't be doing anything too badly wrong,' he said with another twinge of guilt.

She sighed. 'Oh, I wouldn't be too sure. I think I'm just too honest, but at least I'll stand or fall on my own merits, and if anybody gives me a job, they'll know what they're getting. Trouble, probably!'

Her laugh was a little too taut, and the remark puzzled him, but he was distracted by her hand sliding over her hair, nervously checking that it was in place, scraped back against her well-shaped head and twisted into a knot skewered with what looked for all the world like a pair of short chopsticks.

He wondered what would happen if he pulled them out, if the sleek, glossy hair with its paler streaks of gold would fall down round her shoulders in a shimmering curtain, or if it would curl rebelliously. Curl, he thought hopefully, but he was distracted again by her hand moving down, straightening the lapel of her jacket, tugging at her skirt as if to lengthen it. The hem skimmed her slender, shapely knees, and he felt a little surge of jealousy that it wasn't his hand running over her thigh like that…

Good grief. What was happening to him? He hadn't reacted like this to a woman in years.

'You look fine,' he said hastily. 'Stop worrying. Very

chic and professional. I have to go, they'll be waiting for me. Just remember to smile.'

'Thanks. Good luck.' She grinned a little off-kilter, her eyes slightly less wary, and then, just as he turned to go, she threw him a curve.

'Would you give me the job?' she asked, and this time he couldn't lie. He felt his mouth tug into a smile.

'Absolutely.'

Bless his heart, she thought ruefully. If only!

He waggled his fingers at her, turned and strode down the corridor, palming the double doors out of the way as she watched him go. She tried—she really tried—to wish him positive vibes, but it was hard. She wanted this job so much and he was, after all, her competition.

But then the door at the end of the corridor opened, and she heard a man's voice—the great Mr Douglas?—say casually, 'Hi, there. Good of you to join us.'

She didn't hear his reply, because the door swooshed shut behind him, but she'd heard enough. She turned back to the window, staring out over the car park and the trees in the distance, her optimism fading even further. He knew them. No wonder he'd gone breezing down there without a care in the world, whereas she was hovering out here, a bundle of nerves.

'Dr Spicer? Could you come through?'

So soon? It must be just a formality, then, a foregone conclusion. Damn, damn and double damn.

She nearly told the secretary, Maggie, that she wouldn't waste their time, but Maggie smiled at her and held the door, and that didn't seem to leave her a lot of choice.

Oh, well, it couldn't get worse than being told she hadn't got it. She straightened her shoulders, swallowed hard and dredged around for an answering smile. Not easy, but she managed it, and even hung on to it until Maggie opened the door and she was ushered in, but then it failed her.

There were three of them, two men, one woman, seated around a table, and there was one empty chair.

'Dr Spicer, thank you for joining us,' the woman at the head of the table was saying, but she wasn't really listening, because there, on the left of the empty chair, was her fellow interviewee, getting to his feet with lazy grace and smiling at her.

She would have thought they'd show him out first, give her the dignity of a private rejection—but then he walked towards her, his hand outstretched and his smiled tinged with apology, and said, 'Hugh Douglas. Welcome to the Audley Memorial Hospital, Dr Spicer,' and she wasn't sure whether to cry or hit him.

His hand was still extended, and for a moment she contemplated ignoring it and slapping him instead. Only for a moment, though—just long enough to make him think.

Then tipping back her head and meeting his eyes again with a look that should have fried his eyeballs, she said, softly but clearly, 'Well. Fancy meeting you here, *Mr Douglas.*' And instead of slapping that guilty, handsome face, she placed her hand in his for the second time that morning.

His fingers closed around hers and his mouth twitched. 'I'm sorry. I owe you an apology.'

'I think so. I don't like being made a fool of—and I hate being lied to.'

Her voice was deathly quiet, and his reply was just as

quiet. 'I don't recall making a fool of you, Eve—and I didn't lie, exactly. I meant every word I said.'

She extracted her hand from his. '*Every* word?' Even the bit about giving her the job? But his smile had faded and his eyes were utterly sincere.

'*Absolutely,*' he repeated. Funny, it was harder to believe him this time, no matter how much she might want to.

'I'm sorry, have we missed something?' The woman at the head of the table interrupted their soft-voiced exchange. 'Do you two know each other? Because if there's a conflict of interest here, Mr Douglas, we ought to know.'

'No conflict, Julia,' he said easily. 'We met a few moments ago at the top of the stairs. I wasn't perhaps quite fair with her about my identity. Hopefully she won't hold it against me.'

Eve felt her eyes drawn to him again—the lean, muscled frame that did incredible things to his understated charcoal-grey suit, the warmth in his toffee-brown eyes, the teasing smile that played at the corners of his mouth—and refused to allow herself to contemplate holding anything against Hugh Douglas—least of all herself!

'Eve, allow me to introduce you to my colleagues,' he went on smoothly. 'Dr Julia Fry, our fertility expert, and Sam Gregory, another of the obs and gynae consultants.'

She shook their hands, noting that Julia's was cool and hard—curiously like her eyes—and that Sam's was warm and firm and matched his smile.

So it was Julia she was going to have to convince.

Hugh Douglas drew out her chair, turned the full wattage of his charm on her with a smile that made her knees go weak and slid the chair in behind her in the nick of time, bending so his breath whispered over the nape of her neck.

'Break a leg,' he murmured, so low that only she could hear it, and she wondered if he realised it wasn't *her* leg she was contemplating breaking!

As he hooked his own chair back in behind him and sat down again, she took a steadying breath, smiled again and swept her eyes around the table, wondering who was going to start.

She didn't have long to wait. 'Thank you for seeing us at such short notice,' Hugh Douglas said, and she turned to him, her smile taking on a cynical twist that she could feel but couldn't control.

'No problem. As you'll be aware, I'm not in a post at the moment—'

'No, I noticed that in your CV,' Julia Fry said, her expression chilly, as if she still didn't quite trust what was going on. 'As you know, we only have the post because the person we'd appointed has had an accident and is on long-term sick leave, but we weren't expecting to find anyone of the right calibre able to take it on at such short notice. Perhaps you could explain your immediate availability, Dr Spicer?'

Here we go, she thought, and swallowed discreetly. 'I shouldn't have been available. I was offered a post, but the offer was subsequently withdrawn just before I was due to start, so I missed the February rotation start date—hence I'm applying for locum posts.'

'Why was the offer withdrawn?' That was Sam Gregory coming in unexpectedly, studying her over his steepled fingers, asking the very question she'd fruitlessly hoped to avoid, but his eyes were kind and his tone encouraging.

'It was...personal.'

'I think we have a right to an explanation, if you wish us to consider your application seriously, Dr Spicer,' Julia Fry said without a trace of warmth, and Eve's heart sank. 'It is, after all, almost April and you're still without a job.'

Eve met Julia's eyes full on and sighed softly, resigning herself to another lost opportunity, another interview down the pan. 'Of course. He was a friend of my father's. He has a good reputation as a surgeon, and that was why I'd applied. However, he also has a reputation as a womaniser, but I'd fondly imagined that his relationship with my father might protect me from that. Apparently not. I complained to him, and he withdrew the offer. Said I was a troublemaker.'

'And are you?'

'No. Not if my colleagues don't grope me uninvited.'

There was a grunt of laughter from her left, quickly stifled, and she was aware of Sam shifting, leaning back, relaxing and enjoying the moment.

She wished she had that luxury, but Julia's eyes sharpened and she shot a look at Hugh that should have withered him.

Apparently he was made of sterner stuff. 'I can promise you that won't happen here, Dr Spicer,' he cut in. 'Whatever the reason, their loss is our gain and you're available.' Leaning forward, the laughter slowly fading from his eyes to be replaced by something much more searching, he continued, 'Now, earlier you said you'd get this job on your own merits and if anyone gave you a job they'd know what they were getting. So, Dr Spicer, what would we be getting?'

Apart from trouble, he could have added, and she wanted to shoot herself for having been quite so horribly honest earlier.

She wondered if he'd even remembered her saying it, but one look into his twinkling eyes and she knew perfectly well that he did. Oh, damn.

She couldn't allow herself to be distracted by his mischievous smile or that wicked twinkle in his warm brown eyes. He was as devious as a snake, albeit a sexy, well-made and highly desirable snake, but he held her future in his hands, and she couldn't afford to lose this opportunity, so she sucked in a deep breath and launched on her sales pitch.

'Dedication,' she said. 'Concentration, attention to detail, a willingness to learn, good basic surgical skills and a sound foundation. I like people, I try and get on with them, and I'm good at assessing situations quickly. My diagnostic skills are showing promise, and although I haven't done very much in the way of obstetrics, I've prepared for it with a great deal of reading and I'm keen to get some hands-on experience to back it up. I'm not always a very good judge of character, though, and I tend to be a little too trusting, but I'm working on that.'

She met Hugh's eyes and he had the grace to look uncomfortable, but he didn't look away. She had to give him credit for that.

'That was slick—it sounds as if you've had a great deal of interview practice,' Julia put in, breaking the rather awkward silence.

Eve felt the barb sink in.

'Unfortunately, rather more than I would have liked,' she said honestly, and she caught a gleam of approval in Hugh's eye.

'Nothing wrong with being prepared,' Sam said, defending her unexpectedly, and Julia gave him a chilling look before turning back to continue her grilling.

'And where do you see yourself in the future?' she went on, looking broadly unimpressed by all of them.

'As a consultant at thirty-two,' Eve said, going for broke. If she could ever get off the interview bandwagon…

'So—a career doctor. In obstetrics?'

'Or a related field, yes.'

'Why obstetrics?' Sam asked, and she felt herself relax a little. This she knew.

'Because the patients tend to be well, and you're helping them do something that comes naturally. That has to be a refreshing change from general surgery, which was my last rotation. And I love babies.'

'So why not midwifery instead of medicine?' Julia asked. 'We tend to see women when things go wrong. Have you thought of that? In my job I see women because things *aren't* happening naturally, and I know many of our maternity patients are less than well.'

'Of course—and part of the job, surely, is to put that right as much as possible so they can have the families they want.'

'But it doesn't always work.'

'Well, it can't work at all if there aren't doctors doing it,' she retorted, and she saw Sam's mouth tilt into an approving smile.

Hugh was looking thoughtful, though. 'So much for obstetrics. What about gynae?' he asked. 'If you don't like sick people, you may not like gynae, and the two disciplines tend to go hand in hand. I wonder if you've considered that deeply enough.'

'Absolutely!' she protested, mentally kicking herself.

She'd walked into that one with her eyes wide open, and now they thought she didn't like medicine! 'And I didn't say I didn't like sick people. That's the other side of the coin, and why I went into medicine. Why I would choose this branch over any other is because it can bring so much joy into people's lives, and if I can be a part of that, I don't see that it's anything to apologise for. And for the record I definitely see myself as a doctor and not as a midwife. I haven't spent the last ten years getting to this point to realise I'm barking up the wrong tree so, please, don't imagine that.'

'Have you ever lost a patient, Dr Spicer?' Julia cut in. 'Because, in our field, if you aren't careful, you can easily lose two, and I wonder if you're tough enough to take that. Are you sure this area of medicine is what you really want to be doing with your life, or would you actually be better headed for general practice?'

Oh, lord, the woman definitely hated her, and Hugh thought she was a silly little optimist. Damn. Resigning herself to failure—again—she tried to find an intelligent and comprehensive answer, and wondered how long they'd torture her before they told her someone else was getting the job.

'I think we should give her the post.'

'What about Dr Meadows?' Julia said. 'He was good.'

'David Meadows was arrogant and opinionated. Eve Spicer isn't arrogant.'

'We all know what you see in her, Hugh,' Julia said a touch shrewishly, and he had to bite his tongue. Ever since she'd come on to him six months ago and he'd gently but firmly turned her down, she'd been distinctly chilly towards him. This time, though, he wasn't going to make any concessions to her hurt pride. It was his post, his registrar's job, and he had the final say. Besides, he could still hear Eve saying she'd lost the last two posts to a man. Well, not this time, not if he had anything to do with it—and he did.

'I want her,' he said, meeting Julia's eyes straight on, 'and I intend to have her.'

'I don't doubt it,' Sam murmured, just too low for Julia to catch, but she shot him a quelling look nonetheless.

'Oh, well, be it on your own head. I don't think she had enough confidence but, no doubt, with your hand to guide her, she'll come on in leaps and bounds. Her last post seems to have gone well, and her references are certainly excellent, but I'm concerned about her attitude to sick people. I hope she doesn't think this is going to be all cooing babies and happy mums, because she's in for a rude shock. And I'm also worried about this sexual harassment thing. Just make sure your hands are only guiding her surgical skills.'

'I don't think we need to worry about that,' he said bluntly. 'I don't mix business with pleasure—as you well know.'

The remark hit home, and Julia sucked in her breath. Sam looked away, and Julia glared at Hugh, shoved back her chair and stood up, her furious eyes skewering him. Hell hath no fury, he thought, and braced himself, but it was a dignified if ruffled retreat. For now.

Her voice was crisp. 'Well, you've obviously made your mind up. Have her if you want her. I just hope you don't regret it.'

'I do want her—and I won't regret it,' he said, hoping to heaven he was right, and turned to Sam. 'If you agree?'

'Excellent choice,' Sam said, not bothering to hide his smile. 'I liked her, too—nice, uncomplicated girl, and her academic record is stunning. If her practical skills match up she'll do well, I think.'

'I think so. I'll go and call her in—and I'll try and resist the urge to grope her on the way back,' he said drily, drawing a huff of outrage from Julia which he ignored with the ease of long practice.

He stood up, opened the door and forced himself to walk slowly down the corridor. He pushed the door open, caught Eve staring nervously out over the car park with her hands locked together, and as she turned, he felt desire kick him firmly and unexpectedly in the groin.

'Dr Spicer?'

'I know,' she said, her eyes resigned. 'You would have given me the job, but it was out of your hands…'

He grinned, taken with her honesty, which managed to struggle to the surface despite the nerves. He admired that immensely. Real guts. 'Not at all,' he hastened to assure her. 'If you want the job, it's yours—but you'd better come back and let Julia Fry make you the offer, or she'll get all bent out of shape and we couldn't have that, now, could we?'

Her jaw dropped. 'Me?' she whispered, then her voice changed to a little shriek and she threw herself into his arms and—hugged him!

Dammit, she actually hugged him, pressing that delectable little body firmly up against his and squeezing the life out of him. So much for sexual harassment! Then abruptly she let him go, coloured furiously and pressed her hands to her face.

'Oh, I'm so sorry! I can't believe I did that.'

'Forget it,' he said, wondering if he ever would, but her eyes were searching his as if it still hadn't sunk in.

'Are you sure? Really? I got the job?'

Her eyes were sparkling with tears of joy, and he had to bite the insides of his cheeks to keep the smile in. 'Really, Eve. If you can do it at such short notice, we'd like you to start on Monday.'

'Monday! Oh, thank you so much! Oh, good grief! I can't believe it, especially after that rubbish about liking obs because people are well. You must think I'm a complete airhead—I can't believe you still want me.'

'Oh, we still want you,' he said, wondering if it was as obvious as it felt.

'You won't be sorry. I promise I won't let you down.'

'I'm sure you won't,' he said, his own smile refusing to stay trapped in the face of such enthusiasm. 'Come on, let's go and do this properly.'

He ushered her through the door, manfully resisting the urge to put his hand on that delicate hollow in the small of her back and wondered how in the hell he was going to keep his hands to himself while he was working with her. No wonder the old professor had succumbed to temptation. The woman was enough to tempt a saint, and Hugh hadn't been a saint in his entire life. He was just too busy to do anything about it, and now was certainly *not* the time!

Eve couldn't believe she'd *done* that!

Flung her arms round him and hugged him, for goodness' sake!

Madness. Of all the undignified, stupid things to do—but it hadn't been the great Hugh Douglas she'd been hugging it had been the man she'd met before, the man who'd smiled at her and put her at her ease, who'd said he'd give her the job—and had, bless his heart.

And all that talk about the professor groping her, and she'd gone and flung her arms round him and squashed herself all over him like a rash!

She groaned inwardly, wondering if it was too late for him to change his mind because of her stupidity, but he didn't seem inclined to dither, just strode down the corridor, ushered her back into the room and stood there without contradicting while Julia offered her the job and welcomed her to the department.

So it was real.

She couldn't believe it. She'd actually got the job! Even if it wasn't a unanimous verdict, which it clearly wasn't. Julia, summoning a smile that was meant to be welcoming but failed, shook her hand and congratulated her.

Sam, warm, generous and much more genuine in his welcome, did the same.

And then Hugh pulled his bleep out of his pocket, frowned at it and excused himself.

'So, Dr Spicer—will you be able to start on Monday?' Julia asked, and Eve nodded.

'Yes. It'll be a bit of a rush, but so long as I can sort accommodation—'

'You can stay with us for a bit if necessary,' Sam volunteered. 'If you can stand the kids. I'll prime Molly to look out for you, so you can meet her. She's a midwife in the department. She's easy to spot—she's waddling at the moment.'

'Waddling?'

'Thirty-four weeks down, six to go.'

'Ah,' she said, answering his wry smile. 'That kind of waddling.'

The door opened and closed behind her, and without preamble Hugh said, 'Eve, what are you doing now?'

'I don't know—nothing. Why?' she asked, puzzled. Was this his way of dismissing her?

Apparently not. 'My SHO's off sick and my specialist registrar's running my antenatal clinic. He's just seen one of my mums and he's worried—query antepartum haemorrhage from a placenta previa. He's sending her up to Theatre as a precaution and I need to get up there fast. If I have to do a section I'll need an assistant and he's up to his eyes. Want to scrub in and help me?'

She felt her eyes widen. 'Me?'

'If you have time.'

She swallowed, then nodded. 'Um...sure. I only put two hours on my car park ticket, though.'

'Don't worry about that. It'll be fine. Come on—we need to hurry.'

'What about insurance and stuff? I mean, I'm not on contract till Monday.'

'Hugh, this is most irregular.'

'You want the baby to die, Julia? Sam, fix it, please. Locum or something?'

'Consider it done,' Sam said, and that was that.

Hugh whisked her up to the theatre suite, threw a set of theatre blues at her and pointed her towards the female changing room. Then, without bothering to move, he stripped off his clothes and tugged on the scrubs right then and there.

Oh, boy. She tried not to look. She really, *really* tried

not to look, but he was just too gorgeous to miss, all that hard, lean muscle and his legs—oh, lord, his legs…

'Boots or clogs are over here, help yourself to any that haven't got a name on. Here—have a locker for your things,' he said, pointing out a spare one, and she forgot about his body and shot into the changing room, ridding herself of the strangling suit and hated tights and diving into the top, pulling up the trousers of the scrubs, tightening the drawstring with fingers that were starting to tremble.

Was this op part of the interview? she wondered as she stuffed her clothes into the locker. Another sneaky, devious test, like their little chat at the top of the stairs? No. She'd been offered the job. They couldn't take it away, could they? Although the professor had, but she'd been on the point of lodging an official complaint about him, so it hadn't been surprising.

As for the pre-interview subterfuge, she was still contemplating whether or not to forgive Hugh when their patient was wheeled in, eyes fearful even though she was clearly trying not to panic, and Eve forgot all about it, her attention totally engaged by the way he soothed and calmed his patient with his gentle manner and a few reassuring words.

'Trying to keep me on my toes, Jeannie?' he said with a wry grin, his hands already moving over her, asking for details, nodding as he heard them.

Her pulse was up, her blood pressure down, she was on 100 per cent oxygen to help the baby and for now, at least, the little one seemed to be OK. They could hear the foetal heartbeat on the monitor, sounding very fast to Eve's ears, and the monitor showed the heart rate to be over 150. The baby was tachycardic, and if it wasn't delivered soon, it would be in real trouble. At thirty-seven weeks it was certainly viable and would probably be fine without any extra help or support—so long as they could get it out soon enough.

Eve watched Hugh examine the patient quickly, confirming what they already knew from the information he'd been given, then he straightened up, the woman's hand in his.

'OK, Jeannie, let's get this baby out for you now. Paul, I'm sorry, you're going to have to wait outside, but it won't be long and we'll bring the baby out to you as soon as possible.'

The husband nodded nervously, and as the anaesthetist started to work on Jeannie, Hugh scrubbed, held his arms out for the gown, snapped on his gloves and headed for the operating room, with Eve scarcely a second behind him.

'Right, let's move,' he said. 'Knife?'

Jeannie was draped and ready, and with the first slice of the blade Eve felt the tension rise.

'This shouldn't be too hard, because the placenta's lying against the back wall, so at least I won't have to go through it—OK, suction please—Eve, can you hold the retractors? Thank you. Fundal pressure, please.'

And in a whoosh of blood and amniotic fluid he eased the baby out and handed her to the waiting neonatal team, clamping and cutting the cord without delay. As the baby was carried off, a furious little wail from her brought a sigh of relief from everyone.

Except Hugh. He was stern-faced and silent, bar the odd snapped instruction for syntocinon or suction, and as Eve assisted he scooped out the placenta, dropped it in a bowl and the well of blood slowed to a trickle.

Then he let his breath out on a sigh, his shoulders dropped and he grinned, his eyes crinkling over his mask.

'That's got it,' he said, and everyone relaxed.

Everyone, that is, except Eve, because with the next breath he said, 'OK. I'm happy with that. You can close. Let's see your suturing at first hand. This is Eve, by the way, everybody. My new registrar. Dr Spicer, meet the team.'

There were a few polite murmurs of welcome, and that was it. In at the deep end. But he kept his mouth shut for the most part while she sutured, and she forgot about him after the first couple of stitches and just got on with it, following his suggestions for the kind of closure to use for each layer. Finally she was done.

'Well done, very neat,' he said as she snipped the last suture. She looked up into his gorgeous brown eyes and they locked with hers and she was suddenly thrown into confusion, her smile fading. Something fierce and elemental and dangerous crackled between them, nearly taking her legs out from under her, and she wondered if she wouldn't have been safer with the old professor's roaming hands.

Then he stepped back, tugged off his gloves and mask, dropped them in the bin with his gown and turned to her with a smile, his eyes back to normal so she wondered if she'd imagined it.

'Come on. Let's go and see the proud father and have a look at this baby. Then I owe you lunch—and since I haven't even had breakfast yet, I won't take no for an answer.'

Oh, yes. Much, much safer with the old professor. Apart from anything else, she could outrun him, and she had a horrible feeling that the only direction she wanted to run in with Hugh was straight back into his arms!

And there was no way on God's green earth that *that* was going to happen.

CHAPTER TWO

'WHY didn't you tell me who you were?'

Hugh paused, his fork hovering in front of his mouth, and met her eyes over the salad. 'I don't know. I just wanted to talk to you without you knowing who I was—get a glimpse of the real you. And, anyway, hearing about my great reputation did wonders for my ego.'

Eve groaned and coloured fiercely, burying her face in her hands and shaking her head from side to side, so that the loose, soft curls—yes!—swirled around her shoulders like waves breaking on a shore.

'You are a louse—even if you are my boss and I shouldn't say that.'

He dragged his eyes off her hair and pulled a rueful face. 'Say what you like. I agree. I shouldn't have done it, and I'm sorry, but I'd probably do it again.'

She grinned, a wry, twisted little grin full of understanding. 'Why doesn't that surprise me?' She sipped her drink, poked a bit of lettuce around her plate and looked up at him again. 'Do you think the bright theatre lights hurt babies' eyes?'

The question surprised him but, then, he was beginning

to learn that his new registrar was full of surprises. 'Possibly. I like all the deliveries in my charge to be done in the lowest practical light, so the babies aren't blinded. I'd hate to think their first view of the world damaged them in any way, but it isn't always possible.'

'Does it? Damage them?'

He shrugged. 'I don't know. I just think it's unnatural, and even with an intervention like a section I like to make it as natural and quiet as possible, which it usually is for an elective procedure. This kind of thing's different. It's bad enough that the mother isn't conscious and can't bond with the baby immediately, but, in the case of an antepartum haemorrhage, it all gets a bit frantic. With an APH there isn't time to worry about anything but getting the baby out fast and getting control of the bleeding. There certainly isn't time for niceties.'

She nodded slowly. 'No, there isn't, but I agree with you about keeping it nice and natural as far as one can. That makes sense.'

'I try to. It can be hard. So much of what filters through to me is tricky. I only get them if it's gone wrong, and by definition that means it's not straighforward.'

'Like Jeannie?'

'Like Jeannie,' he agreed. 'But that could have been much worse. The placental separation was only slight and the syntocinon she'd been given had almost stopped the haemorrhage. And the position of the placenta helped. If it's across the front of the uterus we have to go in a different way, making it up as we go along, really, and that can be much harder in an emergency. She was lucky. They both were.'

His bleep interrupted them, and he pulled it out of his pocket, frowned at it and wondered if he could leave his specialist registrar to manage.

Probably not, unless he was going to abandon the clinic patients for hours, and tempting though it was…

'That's Oliver again. I'm going to have to go. My clinic's overrunning, and if we don't get on top of it my afternoon list will be delayed. I'll see you on Monday—and if there's anything else you want to know, ask Maggie. She's expecting you this afternoon—you need to sign a locum form, I expect, for today, and then she'll give you a guided tour and answer your questions. And when you're done with Maggie, Molly Gregory, Sam's wife, wants to meet you and she'll give you the midwife's side of it. She's also one of my mums, so take note. We'll be delivering her soon.'

'Sam said something about kids at home. Is it their third or something?'

He laughed. 'Or something's just about it. Their fourth, but it's more complicated than that. She's a fascinating woman. She'll probably tell you all about herself.' He drained his coffee, stood up and held out his hand. 'It's good to have you on board, Eve,' he said, and felt the warm touch of her fingers all the way to his soul.

He had the hardest job letting go.

After her whirlwind tour of the hospital with Maggie, Hugh's secretary, she was handed over to Molly Gregory for a slower, more in-depth tour of Maternity.

Slower because, apart from any other consideration, Molly was, as Sam had said, waddling just a little.

'When's it due?' Eve asked her sympathetically, although Sam had already told her.

Molly gave a wry grin and sighed. 'Five weeks and six days. I can't wait. I thought it would be fine because I'm only working part time, but struggling around on the floor—'

'The floor?' Eve said, puzzled, and Molly laughed.

'When did you last see a normal, natural birth?'

'Um—probably ages ago,' Eve confessed, and Molly patted her hand.

'Don't worry. I'll try and make sure you get to see plenty before I vanish on maternity leave in a fortnight, so Hugh doesn't spend his entire time filling your head with interventionist ideas.'

'Is he likely to?'

Molly chuckled. 'No, not really. He does everything he can to let people give birth without interference, to the point when even I might be starting to worry, but he's like Sam—in there and sorting it fast when it needs it. And he's got an excellent safety track record, so I'm inclined to trust him.'

'Do you work with Sam?' she asked, curious about their work-home partnership, and Molly laughed again, shaking her head.

'Not if I can help it. We just take it home if we do, and carry on arguing over the supper table. Mostly we agree, and Sam's a fantastic doctor, but, then, I'm biased.'

'You should be, as he's your husband,' Eve said with a smile, and Molly chuckled.

'Probably. We go back a long way. Did Hugh tell you?'

She shook her head. 'No. He said you were a fascinating woman and you'd tell me yourself.'

'Fascinating?' She smiled. 'Maybe. I've had two babies

for other people—carried implanted embryos for them. The second was for Sam and his first wife.'

Eve felt her jaw sag, and hastily recovered herself. 'Really? How incredible—I've never met a surrogate mother before.'

'Well, you have now. And it was amazing. A bit hard at the end—especially with Jack. I really didn't want to hand him over, but when they put him in Sam's arms…' She shrugged. 'Somehow it all seemed right then. I knew he'd be OK with Sam.'

But not the mother. How interesting—and also interesting that she sounded like she'd been in love with Sam even at that point, although she hadn't said so in as many words. But to hand over the baby…

She gave a little shiver. 'I can't imagine going through all that and giving my baby away.'

'It wasn't my baby. I said that over and over again, both times, and it was the only thing that got me through it some days. The first time I didn't know if I could, but my own daughter Libby had brought me and my husband so much joy, and when he died, I thought it was something I could do for someone else. So I had Laura, and Libby knew all about her, and we're still in touch, so it was OK.'

'So how did Sam find out about you being a surrogate mother? Did you work together?'

'No, not then. I met him when I visited another surrogate mum in hospital. She was his patient, and he'd talked to her about it. His wife couldn't carry a child, but was desperate, he said, and she'd asked him to make enquiries. And that was it. I agreed, stupidly fell in love with him, gave him his child and tried to put it out of my mind. But I could never forget Jack—or Sam. And then he started working here, and we met again, and that was it. His wife had died in an accident, I'd been widowed for years, and we were both free. It seemed the obvious thing to do, to get married, and then we had Bonnie. She's two now.'

'And now you're having another one, which will be your…' she did a quick mental tot-up '…fifth pregnancy?'

Molly groaned and chuckled. 'For my sins. My poor old body will never be the same again.' But she said it cheerfully, as if it didn't really matter, not compared to the joy of bringing a child into the world, and Eve felt a little lump forming in her throat.

One day, she promised herself. Only a few more years, a few more mountains to climb, a few more targets to meet, and she could think about it. She'd have her family one day, when she was ready, but in the meantime she was a doctor, and for now that was more than enough to make her happy.

'And Hugh's in charge of your antenatal care?' she said, getting back to business.

'Yes, poor man,' Molly said with another smile. 'I wouldn't want his job, not with Sam hovering over him and checking every decision he makes. I'll have to make sure I have a nice, uncomplicated delivery when you're on duty, so you can come and enjoy it and have a bit of light relief. Talking of which, fancy a cup of tea? I'm off duty now, and the kids are taken care of, so for once I've actually got time to sit down and have a civilised conversation.'

Eve nodded. 'That would be wonderful. In fact, if you can tell me anything about where I should live and how I go about finding an appropriate letting agent, it would be fantastic, because I've got to get somewhere by Monday, and although Sam was kind enough to offer to let me stay with you— Did you know that, by the way?' Molly smiled and nodded, and Eve continued, 'I think you've probably got enough on your plate and, anyway, I'd quite like to get sorted. Being officially homeless is very unsettling.'

'Oh, I agree. Although you're more than welcome, but it's not the same as a place of your own, and the kids are a bit full on until you're used to them. Let me get my bag and we'll go and grab the paper from the newsagent's in Reception and study it. It's property day today and there's usually a big rental section. You might be lucky and find something straight away.'

So that was it. They settled down over tea and pored over the adverts, and Molly told her about the various areas, and within half an hour she had an appointment with an agent to view a river-front apartment with a balcony and dedicated parking.

It wasn't cheap, but it sounded lovely and it sounded safe and it was five minutes from the hospital, and they were all high on her list of priorities. Apart from which, it was available immediately.

She took it, one glance at the flat enough to convince her, and by the end of the day she had a new job, a new home and, in Molly, a new friend.

Not a bad day's work, she thought, and then drove back to her brother's house, packed up all her possessions and drove back to Audley the following day, Friday, collected the key from the letting agent, signed all the legal stuff and moved into her new home with a huge sigh of relief.

Finally, after the hell of the last two months, her life was back on track, and for the first time in ages she was actually looking forward to the future.

* * *

Hugh spent the weekend tearing his hair out.

The kids were a nightmare—no surprises there, then, and when had parenting ever been easy?—and when he finally got ten minutes to himself late on Sunday afternoon he stuck his head out into the garden and realised that the winter had gone, spring was here and the weeds were having a field day.

Good. He could get stuck into them, rip them all out and burn off a bit of his frustration.

'Dad? There's someone called Eve on the phone for you,' his daughter Lucy yelled through the window, and he stripped off his gardening gloves and went back in, shocked at his eagerness.

'Eve?' he said, picking up the receiver, and her voice, soft and hesitant, came down the line and went straight to his heart—literally. His pulse speeded up, he felt the pounding in his neck, in his head— Damn. Everywhere!

So much for dealing with his frustration!

'I'm so sorry to ring you at home, but with the short notice and everything we didn't really arrange when and where I should find you tomorrow. I got your number from Molly Gregory. She suggested I ring you. I hope that's OK?'

'Of course it is.' More than OK. It was bloody fantastic, and if he'd had a working brain left that fact would have worried him sick, but he was too busy listening to her voice to listen to reason. 'Look, this is probably too short notice, because I expect you're still unpacking and settling in, but are you doing anything this evening?'

Her laugh was music to his ears. 'No. There's a limit to how long it takes to arrange the few things you can get in a car and I've been here since Friday. Why?'

'I thought you could come round here for supper, and we could talk through anything you're worried or unsure about.' And he could get to see her again, without an audience, because the kids were going out and he'd have the place to himself.

He felt his gut tighten with anticipation, and held his breath waiting for her reply.

'Oh. Well—that would be lovely,' she said. 'If you're sure? It's not very much notice.'

'It's enough, if you don't expect cordon bleu. Seven?'

'Fine.'

He gave her the address and directions, and as he cradled the phone, a silly smile tugging at his lips, Lucy said, 'So who's Eve, then?'

He jerked up straight, then rammed his hands in his pockets, wandered over to the fridge and opened the door, trying hard to school his expression and look casual. 'My new registrar. She's coming over to talk shop.'

'Yeah, right.'

'Yes,' he said firmly. 'And we could do with some peace. Still want to go to Amy's?'

'You said I couldn't! You said I had to stay in and get an early night.'

'I've changed my mind. You can have an early night at Amy's.'

She snorted, and he levelled a finger at her. 'Don't push it. I just want a chance to talk to Eve without constant interruptions and arguments, and if you get to spend the evening with Amy on the back of it, if you've got any sense, you'll shut up and take advantage of it. All right?'

'All *right*!' she said with a grin, and went out chanting, 'Dad fancies Eve, Dad fancies Eve.'

'Who's Eve?' Tom asked, strolling in and looking deeply curious.

Hugh scrubbed his hand round the back of his neck and scowled at his daughter's retreating back.

'My new registrar—and I do *not* fancy her!' he retorted, conscious of the lie but deeply unwilling to lay himself bare to his increasingly hard-to-fool children. Lord, was nothing sacred?

'Whatever,' Tom said. 'Can I stay at Kelly's tonight?'

'No. You've got school tomorrow, and you've got exams coming up after Easter.'

'Dad, they're months away.'

'Not that long.'

'Well, can Kelly stay the night, then?'

'What—here?'

'Yes, here.'

He gave up and shut the fridge door. 'No. You can go out with her this evening, and then when you leave whichever pub you're taking her to, you can drive her home and come back.'

'Yeah, but that's the thing, you see, Dad. It's Rick's birthday and I want to have a drink and I can't if I'm driving.'

'Then you'll have to put Kelly in a taxi or walk her home.'

'Why can't she just stay here?'

'Because you have to go to school tomorrow and, whatever you say, I know you haven't got all your stuff ready and haven't finished your homework. And, besides, I've got better things to do all night than listen to creaking boards while you two sneak around.'

'Sneak around?' His son sat down at the kitchen table and laughed at him. 'You really think whether she stays here or not makes any difference? Get real, Dad. I'm nearly eighteen. Wake up and smell the coffee.'

And he walked out, leaving Hugh staring after him, his heart sinking.

History repeating itself?

Wake up and smell the coffee, indeed! He swore softly but comprehensively, yanked the fridge door open again and stared blindly at the contents. Why on earth had he complicated things so much by asking Eve to come here? He could have gone to her, met her somewhere, taken her out for dinner…

No. That was even more complicating. This could at least be passed off as two colleagues getting together to discuss work issues.

And pigs flew.

He snatched Parmesan cheese, a bag of peppers, a red onion, some cherry tomatoes and a bag of frilly lettuce from the fridge, shut the door and hunted for a new jar of pesto. Keep it simple, he told himself. Pasta in pesto with roasted vegetables and a tossed salad. Simple.

He was rapidly getting the feeling it was the only thing about this day that would be.

Eve checked her notes, checked the road name and drove slowly down the tree-lined street. Here—35, with a light over the front door and clear brass numerals. A big Victorian house, painted a soft yellow, with two gables facing the road and a dark red front door in the centre with a fanlight over the top, it looked smart, but at the same time friendly and welcoming. There was a light on in the hall and it showed off the beautiful old stained-glass panels in the door, obviously of the same period as the house and giving it a wonderfully cosy feel.

She parked the car outside and got out, feeling a little nervous. It was definitely a family house, and she could hear music through the upstairs window on the right.

That sort of music, the sort that only teenagers could bear to listen to. She wondered how old his children were, and what his wife was like, and how she might feel about having a strange woman suddenly foisted on her on a Sunday evening when she'd probably rather sit down with a glass of wine and do nothing.

She told herself that the sensation she was feeling at the thought that Hugh was married couldn't possibly be disappointment; she didn't want to get involved with a man at this stage in her career, especially not her boss.

But there'd been that look they'd exchanged after she'd closed for him on Thursday after Jeannie's operation, a brooding look full of heat and promise and a connection so powerful she couldn't possibly have imagined it.

Could she? But, in any case, there was no way she'd act on it! After the kerfuffle with the professor, her colleagues were way off limits, and as for her boss—well, a married man with a growing family was right off the scale!

'Eve.'

She looked up, saw him standing beside the car, a smile of welcome in his eyes, and she opened the door and got out, glad to see he was dressed as casually as her. She'd wondered if her jeans and jumper would be too low key, but after dithering around with her wardrobe for hours…

'Hi again,' she said, wondering why her heart was suddenly misbehaving. She really needed to listen to her own advice. She wasn't interested in him. At all! She looked around and groped for practicalities. 'Will my car be OK here?'

He shrugged. 'We've got streetlights, it should be fine, but you can put it in the drive if you want. It's up to you, but Tom's going out in a minute and we'll have to shuffle the cars if you do. It's not a problem, though. Want me to get the keys?'

She shook her head and smiled wryly, wondering who Tom was. His son? Surely he wasn't old enough to have a son who was driving already? Heavens, he was wearing well! 'I'm sure it'll be fine,' she replied, dragging her thoughts back to the car parking. 'It looks a deeply respectable neighbourhood.'

He laughed. 'Oh, it is. Frightfully respectable. We lower the tone, I'm afraid. Come on in. It'll be quieter when Tom goes out. We're on our own for the evening, so we should be able to deal with all your questions and I can tell you a bit more about the hospital.'

We as in him and his wife, or we as in him and her, just the two of them?

She felt a flicker of nerves, but it was the two of them, it seemed, because no one else appeared. No wife to greet her in a flurry of expensive perfume and thinly disguised intolerance, and take the edge off this stupid anticipation she was feeling. Unfortunately.

Hugh led her down the hall and past the bottom of the stairs into the kitchen, a lovely bright room with doors opening into the garden. It was a little chaotic, reflecting the clutter of family life, and the notice-board on the wall was overflowing. She wondered who kept track of the family social calendar, and felt sorry for them. It looked a nightmare.

'Have a seat, I just need to put the pasta on. Red, white or something soft?'

'Oh—soft, please, I'm driving.'

He poured her a glass of pressed apple juice, bitty and cloudy and packed with flavour, and she sipped it and made appreciative noises and watched him shred salad and shave Parmesan cheese with a wicked-looking implement.

A younger version of him stuck his head round the door after a couple of minutes, grinned at her and said, 'Hi, there. I'm Tom. You must be the new registrar. Welcome to the madhouse.'

'Thank you.' She returned his smile, registering the fact that Tom *must* be his son, if looks were anything to go by, and apparently old enough to drive, amazing though it seemed. His next words confirmed it.

'I'm off, Dad. I'll leave the car at Kel's and we'll walk into town from there.'

'You come back here tonight,' Hugh said, pointing the cheese slicer at his son, and she guessed she was coming in in the middle of an argument. A prickle of unease settled in her spine, and she shifted in her chair, paying undue attention to her drink.

'Lucy's out for the night,' Tom protested.

'I don't care about that. I'm not talking about your sister, I'm talking about you.'

'Yeah, whatever. See you.'

'Tom, I'm warning you—'

But the front door banged, leaving them in silence, and after a second Hugh sighed heavily, muttered, 'Kids!' under his breath and headed for the fridge.

It could have been a scene from her teens, she thought, and shook off the memory. Her teens weren't something she wanted to dwell on, especially not tonight.

'You OK with pasta and pesto, by the way?' Hugh was saying. 'I meant to ask you earlier.'

She nodded, suddenly terribly conscious of how alone they were, but she needn't have worried, because Hugh seemed to be going out of his way to keep it friendly and casual. He kept a safe, respectable distance, there were no loaded looks and if she'd had the sense to worry about his motives, his manner would have put her at ease immediately.

So she relaxed, and by the time they'd eaten a simple but messy meal of roasted Mediterranean vegetables, springy spaghetti in pesto and disobediently frilly lettuce, their chins were covered in oil and the ice was well and truly broken.

'Sorry, I could have chosen something a little more dignified to eat,' he said with a grin, and then frowned thoughtfully. 'You've got pesto on your chin,' he murmured. For a moment she thought he was going to lean over and wipe it with his napkin, but she collected herself and got there first.

'Better?'

'Fine,' he said, but there was that thing in his eyes again, and casual seemed to have flown right out of the window…

'Coffee?' His eyes were expressionless again, so that once more she wondered if she was imagining it. Silly.

She got her lungs working again and managed a smile. 'That would be lovely. Thanks.'

They adjourned to the sitting room at the front of the house overlooking her perfectly safe car and, prompted by her questions, he talked enthusiastically about the job and his philosophy of childbirth, so that before she knew where she was the clock in the hall was striking twelve.

'Heavens, I'm sorry, I've kept you talking for ages. I'd better go,' she told him, checking her watch in disbelief, and he stood up and showed her to the door, helping her into her coat with hands that very carefully didn't touch her.

Too carefully, or was she imagining things again? Maybe he was getting paranoid about her because of the harassment thing, or maybe he was simply a very nice, very married man and this silly reaction was totally one-sided.

Which would be ideal, and much safer, and absolutely the most sensible thing.

'I'll see you tomorrow,' he murmured, and for a moment she thought he'd swayed towards her, just a fraction. Not far enough to kiss her, but…

No. She was being silly. Definitely silly. She needed to give herself a good talking-to.

She pasted a bright smile on her face. 'Goodnight, Hugh. Thanks for supper. I'll see you at eight.'

'Fine. Sleep well—we've got a busy day.'

And she knew she'd imagined that flicker of something in his eyes. His only interest in her sleeping pattern was professional, and if she carried on like this he'd be accusing *her* of sexual harassment!

She got into her car and drove away, wondering as she went where his wife had been all evening and whether Tom would come home tonight as instructed by his father. Whatever, it wasn't her problem.

When she got home she made herself a cup of fruit tea and took it to bed, looking forward to the time when the weather warmed up enough for her to sit out on her balcony and look at the river. She could see it from where she sat propped up on her pillows, and she turned out the light and stared at it, allowing her mind to empty. She could see lights reflected in the dark water, broken by the ripples, and the effect was soothing and calming.

More than the next day would be, she thought, but she wouldn't allow herself to worry about it, or about her new boss. She was good at her job. She had to be. She wouldn't allow herself to be anything else. And in the meantime she needed sleep.

She set down her cup, snuggled under the covers and was gone in minutes.

Hugh couldn't sleep.

For some reason Eve had got under his skin, making him think crazy and inappropriate thoughts.

Thoughts of her hot and wild under him, her slender legs locked around his waist, her breasts crushed against his chest and her frantic little cries echoing in his ears…

'Oh, *damn!*'

He threw back the covers and strode across the room, grabbing his dressing-gown off the back of the door and slinging it on as he headed for the stairs.

He checked in mid-stride, swivelled and opened Tom's bedroom door, nearly falling headlong over the mess.

No sign of him, at nearly four in the morning with school the next day.

So either he was still out far, far too late, or he had

stayed over at Kelly's. Either way, he would get the benefit of his father's opinion when he next set eyes on him.

Hugh put the kettle on, propped himself against the worktop and stared blindly down the empty drive. Should he ring Tom and ask him just where the *hell* he thought he was? Or wait until tomorrow?

What if he was dead in a ditch, stabbed on the way home by some drunken lunatic?

In which case, ringing him won't achieve anything and you won't bring him back whatever, reason told him pragmatically, but he was past reason. He picked up his phone, called Tom's number and was further frustrated by the fact that the phone was obviously off.

He left a pithy message on his son's voicemail, threw his own phone down on the worktop and made a cup of tea. Not decaf, not herbal, just good old-fashioned caffeinated builder's tea, nice and thick and calculated to keep him awake.

So what? He was awake anyway, what with Eve and Tom doing their best to drive him to distraction. He may as well have a decent cup of tea and enjoy it.

CHAPTER THREE

'FIRST stop, Jeannie,' Hugh said, and led Eve down the ward to a side room tucked in the angle between two bays, pausing at the sink to wash his hands and rub them with alcohol gel, while Eve followed suit without thinking. It made her hands dry and she had to drown them in heavy-duty hand cream every night, but at least that way she wasn't spreading infection, and right now antibiotic-resistant bugs were everybody's nightmare.

'How's she doing?' she asked as she rubbed the gel briskly into her hands.

'She's getting on really well, and the baby's fine. They can go home today, so long as everything looks OK, so we'll just give her the good news.'

The door was open, and Jeannie was propped up in bed breastfeeding her little daughter. As Eve had expected, the baby hadn't needed any extra support, and although she was a dainty little thing, she was in perfect working order and Jeannie was radiant.

'Hi, there,' she said, grinning broadly at them. 'Come to see my little treasure?' She slipped the tip of her little finger into the corner of her baby's mouth, breaking the suction, and eased her away from her breast, sitting her up with her tiny chin cradled in the fork of Jeannie's thumb and forefinger. 'Say hello to Mr Douglas, little one.'

There was a resounding burp, and they all laughed.

'No name yet?'

Jeannie gave a wry chuckle, gently continuing to rub the baby's back. 'We can't agree. I like Eleanor, Paul likes Katherine.'

'You know she'll be Ellie or Kate, don't you?' Hugh said.

'Probably. I don't care. I just want to call her something other than "Baby". It's getting a little ridiculous!'

He laughed with her. 'You'll get there. Can I take her from you for a moment? I just I want to examine Eve's needlework. Have you seen it yet?'

'Mmm. Looks very tidy. Are you Eve? I'm sorry, I didn't really get to meet you properly the other day.'

Eve smiled. 'No, we were all a bit preoccupied. How are you feeling now?'

'Bit sore, but delighted with the baby and hugely relieved that everything went well. Thank you for sewing me up so beautifully.'

'My pleasure,' she said with a smile, delighted that her careful suturing hadn't gone unappreciated, just as Hugh turned round with the baby in his arms.

'Here,' he said, passing Eve the little one with a knowing grin. 'The best bit of the job. Have a cuddle—I know you're dying to.'

She settled the baby securely in her arms, staring down in fascination into the wide blue eyes and perfect features of Jeannie's tiny daughter.

'She's gorgeous,' she murmured, suppressing that little

maternal urge that seemed to flare up every time she held a baby. One day, she told herself. One day in about eight years or so, once she'd achieved what she'd set out to do.

Until then, she'd content herself with doing the best job she could to ensure her patients had safe deliveries, and she'd grab the odd cuddle along the way. For now, at least, that would have to do.

Hugh looked at Eve with the baby cradled in her arms, and the look on her face brought a lump to his throat.

She should have a child, he thought inconsequentially. She'd look so right with a baby at her breast.

No. Don't think about that. Concentrate.

He checked Jeannie's suture line, felt the position of her fundus to make sure her uterus was contracting properly and glanced through her charts.

'Well, that looks absolutely fine, and if Eve can bear to give young Kate or Ellie back to you, we'll go and sort out your discharge letter and you can go home.'

'Today?'

He smiled at her delighted expression. 'If you want to,' he said, knowing what the answer would be. 'Your community midwife will come and check you and make sure everything's OK, and you'll need to have your stitches out this time next week, but I don't see any reason to keep you here. Will you have some help at home?'

She nodded. 'Paul's arranging to have next week off, and my mother's here now and can stay till the weekend, so I'll be fine.'

'Excellent. Right, Eve, give the baby back.' He said it

with a teasing grin, but her answering smile was a little bleak, and he wondered why.

Why obstetrics, really? And why so forlorn?

A broken heart?

He knew all about that and how it hurt. He knew about holding babies and handing them back to their parents, knew the dull ache it could leave when his arms were empty again.

If Eve's heart was broken, she wasn't alone.

'Right. We need to sort the paperwork, then see the other patients. Some of them might be able to go today as well. Then after lunch we've got a clinic starting at one and I'd like to get down there a little early and go through the paperwork.'

They were walking down the ward towards the nursing station, and he was deliberately brisk, but it seemed to do the trick. The melancholy left her eyes, and she quizzed him about their afternoon ahead.

'Obs or gynae clinic?'

'Gynae. There'll be the usual run-of-the-mill things, but there are one or two odd ones I want to look at a bit more closely. I'd like you to do the initial assessments, then go through your findings with me and I'll see anyone I feel is necessary. Happy with that?'

She nodded. 'Fine.'

'They won't all be well, you know,' he warned, wondering what she'd say to that, but she just looked at him, her brows pleating together into a frown.

'I can do sick people, Hugh. I just didn't want to specialise in anything too unrelentingly heart-rending.'

He stopped walking, an almost-forgotten sorrow reaching out to touch him yet again. 'Obstetrics can be heart-rending, Eve. Believe me. If you don't think you can hack it, get out before it's too late to change your mind.'

'I'm not going to change my mind. And I have no intention of going into general practice or retraining as a midwife!'

A grin flickered over his face and was gone. 'Good. Right, where were we? Oh, yes, the clinic. And tomorrow we've got an early day-case list, and on Wednesday we're on take and we've got an elective list as well, so no doubt it'll get even more hectic. Anyone we aren't happy about today we'll admit, and deal with tomorrow at the end of the day-case time.'

'Will there be room on your list?'

He gave a wry laugh. 'Probably not. How late do you work?'

She grinned. 'How late do you want me to work?' she said, and he shook his head.

'Don't ask. There've been nights when I've finished my list at midnight. Let's hope Wednesday isn't one of them. We'll just have to keep our fingers crossed that not too much comes in overnight tomorrow.'

Famous last words, he thought, wading through his clinic at the end of the day.

He'd had a woman with fibroids in the clinic whom he'd admitted for blood transfusion prior to urgent surgery on Wednesday morning, if her haemoglobin level was high enough by then, and now he had a mother up in maternity with early signs of pre-eclampsia that was threatening to escalate, so her community midwife had admitted her. He had a feeling she'd be in Theatre in the morning for a section if her blood pressure didn't respond overnight, in which case Sam would take her as he was on call tomorrow, but if she hung on they might end up with her on Wednesday.

And that was without all the miscarriages that would be admitted overnight for D and C the next day to remove any last products of conception, and women in labour who got into difficulties and needed assistance.

Still, at least he didn't seem to need to spoonfeed Eve. If her first day was anything to go by, she'd been an excellent choice, and would relieve a lot of the pressure on him and Oliver.

And Alison, his SHO, would be relieved to have another woman on the team. Eve was up on the ward at the moment with Alison, checking on the patient with pre-eclampsia, and once she'd done that she'd be heading home like him, leaving Alison and Oliver in charge for the night.

Now he just had Tom to deal with when he got home, and maybe he could catch up on some of the sleep he'd missed last night. He reached for his mobile in his pocket to turn it on and check his messages, and it wasn't there.

Great. Where on earth had he left it?

He went into his office, searched high and low, checked with the ward and again through the clinic, and finally came to the unwelcome conclusion that he'd lost it.

And as it was a PDA—a diary and organiser, as well as a phone—its loss was catastrophic.

He swore, softly but with considerable feeling, and headed for the car. There was nothing he could do about it tonight. He'd looked in the only likely places. He'd just have to report it missing and replace it.

Again.

* * *

'Oh, no.'

'What?'

Alison had lifted a set of patient notes off the corner of the nursing station, and there on the desk was a mobile phone.

'It's Mr Douglas's phone. He's been looking for it everywhere. It's his lifeline—he'll go mad without it.'

Eve hesitated for a second, then picked it up, slipping it into her pocket and giving Alison a carefully neutral smile. 'I'll drop it in to him. I know where he lives.'

And maybe this time she'd get to meet his wife…

She could hear them as she pulled up outside, on the other side of the street.

Hear them, and see them through the kitchen window straight ahead of her, Tom and his father, with the odd interjection from another voice—a girl? His daughter, maybe, or Tom's girlfriend? It sounded too young to be a woman's voice. They were going at each other hammer and tongs, and her heart sank. She really didn't need this.

She was about to head to the front door when she noticed a door on the side of the house that was hanging open. There was no chance they'd hear the doorbell, she realised, and if it hadn't been for the emphasis Alison had placed on getting the phone back to Hugh quickly, nothing would have induced Eve to go in there.

But she had the phone, and he needed it, and so she took a deep breath and tapped on the open door, just as a pretty girl in her early teens flounced down the hall, rolling her eyes in a perfect recreation of Eve at the same age.

'Oh, hi. Can I help you?' she asked, pausing in her tracks.

'Um—I've got Hugh's phone. He left it at the hospital.'

'Oh, great. Are you Eve?'

'Yes.'

'I'm Lucy. He's in the kitchen. Just go in. He's talking to Tom.'

Talking?

Hardly, she thought, but the girl had run upstairs, leaving her with no choice but to deliver the phone personally, so she made her way warily down the hall towards the kitchen.

The door was ajar, and she put her head round it and cleared her throat. 'Um…Hugh?'

He didn't hear her, of course. They were standing practically nose to nose, Hugh only an inch or so taller than his furiously angry son, and as she took a step into the room Tom delivered what was clearly the *coup de grâce.*

'I'm only telling you this because I need your professional advice, so get off your bloody high horse and listen to me! I may have got Kelly pregnant last night!'

You could have heard a pin drop.

Hugh's jaw sagged, he dropped his head forwards into his hands and groaned. 'How?' he mumbled through his fingers.

Tom gave a bitter little laugh. 'The same way you got my mother pregnant, I guess.'

Her heart pounding, Eve backed away, mentally as well as physically. There was no way she needed to hear this. No way. Eve took another step backwards, just as Hugh dragged his hands down his face and caught sight of her.

He stiffened, groaned again and scrubbed one hand round the back of his neck. 'Uh…Eve. Hi.'

'Um…your phone,' she said inadequately, giving a helpless little shrug. 'You left it on the desk and someone put a set of notes on it. Alison said you'd need it. I'm sorry

I just barged in—the door was open. Your daughter said to come through. I, um, I'll go.'

'No—wait. Can you give us a minute?'

'It's OK, I was just dropping it in. I can't stop. I'll see you tomorrow.'

And setting the phone down on the table, she high-tailed it out of the door.

'Eve, wait!'

He caught up with her just as she was getting into her car, his smile rueful and distracted. 'Look, I'm sorry about this.'

'Don't be. These things happen in families.' And she didn't have a family, thank goodness, and she was getting away from his just as fast as she could.

His laugh was harsh and a little ragged. 'Only in mine, it seems. Thanks for bringing me the phone.'

'You're welcome. I'll see you in the morning.'

He frowned. 'Uh—are you doing anything later?'

'Oh. I don't know,' she said, her mind emptying itself of excuses. 'Why?'

He said nothing for a second, then shook his head. 'Nothing. It doesn't matter. I'll see you tomorrow.'

And he turned and went back into the house like a man with the weight of the world on his shoulders.

Eve didn't envy him the conversation that was sure to follow. She thought of Jeannie and her darling little daughter, and wondered what was in store for them as a family fifteen years down the line. Chaos, probably, like Hugh's, like everyone else's that involved teenagers. She shuddered with the memory. It was all too much.

She backed off the drive and left Hugh to his chaos, retreating to her nice, peaceful apartment by the river. It was bliss. No noise, no chaos, just calm and order and tranquillity.

And silence.

'So what happened?'

Tom shrugged. The anger was gone now, and Hugh could see the worry stamped on his son's pale features. 'I'd had too much to drink. I must have done something stupid to the condom—we were mucking about with it, over who— Whatever,' he mumbled, colouring again. 'It tore. I didn't realise till later.'

Hugh ignored the detail in favour of the salient facts. 'When's her next period due?'

Tom shrugged and looked away. 'How should I know? We don't talk about it. She was going to the clinic after school to get morning-after pills, but it was shut. I thought you'd know what to do.'

'You can go to A and E—or I can give her a private prescription, or you can buy them over the counter, but it wouldn't be a bad idea for her to have a quick health check as she's not on the Pill. Whatever, time is of the essence, so I suggest you go and get her and bring her here now.'

'Don't tell her mother.'

'I won't,' Hugh said, 'but I think *you* should—or she should. How old is she?' he asked as an afterthought, suddenly realising he didn't even know the age of the girl his son was sleeping with. If she was under-age…!

'She's seventeen.'

He felt his shoulders drop about six inches, and the tension drained out of him. Still, too many parallels.

'Go and get her, Tom.'

'Dad, don't yell at her.'

'I won't. I promise. Just get her here now—and go via a supermarket and pick up a pregnancy test.'

Tom blinked. 'But it won't show yet, will it?'

'No, of course not—but unless this was the first time, there might be a possibility that she's already pregnant, and there's no way I'm giving her a prescription for a powerful hormonal contraceptive without knowing that.'

'But—'

'Tom, just do it,' he said shortly. 'Don't tell me my job—not if you want my help. Here, you'd better take some money because, knowing you, you won't have enough. And you'd better get a twin pack, she'll need to repeat the test in a few weeks.'

He thrust a twenty-pound note into his son's hand and watched him go, his heart heavy. Of all the messes…

It took Tom over forty minutes to return with a reluctant and clearly very embarrassed Kelly, by which time Hugh had checked his facts on post-coital contraception and armed himself with a blood-pressure monitor and his private prescription pad.

He summoned a smile and gave the nervous, embarrassed teenager a little one-armed hug. 'It's OK, Kelly,' he said gently. 'I'm not going to judge you. Heaven knows, I'm the last person to be able to do that. Just take the pregnancy test and follow the instructions, OK?'

She nodded miserably, disappeared into the cloakroom and Hugh faced Tom squarely.

'So—how are you going to make sure this doesn't happen again?'

Tom swallowed and shook his head. 'I dunno—use thicker condoms?'

'Or she could go on the Pill, or have an implant, get a diaphragm, or an IUCD—'

'What?'

'A coil. A little bit of bent wire that sits inside the uterus and makes the environment hostile to implantation.'

Tom stared at him queasily. 'Dad, I don't do biology and stuff,' he protested, but Hugh shook his head.

'Oh, you do. You do this biology, or you don't engage in sexual activity. You have a duty and a responsibility to protect Kelly from unwanted pregnancy. Knowing how to do that is part of that responsibility.'

Tom nodded, chastened and unhappy. 'OK.'

'Go with her to the sexual health clinic at the hospital, and get this sorted out,' he instructed, but Tom's eyes widened in horror.

'No way! What if someone recognises us?'

'Then they'll work out what you're doing. That's fine. If you're old enough to do this, then you're old enough to do it properly. That means acknowledging your relationship.'

Kelly came back into the room, holding out a little white stick with one blue line on it. 'That's no, isn't it?' she asked uncertainly, and Hugh nodded, immeasurably relieved that it wasn't already too late.

'That's no,' he said, his voice almost a croak of relief. 'Right. Kelly, do you want Tom in here?'

'Do you need to examine me or anything?' she asked, looking worried, but he shook his head.

'I'll take your blood pressure and ask you all sorts of questions, but that's all. It's up to you.'

'He can stay.'

'OK. Sit yourself down—I'll need your arm to check your blood pressure.'

She slid her arm out of her jumper, colouring slightly and tugging the front down to cover her bra. Poor, silly little kids, he thought, and remembered how he'd felt.

Overwhelmed. Overwhelmed by love and guilt and dread and confusion, only for them it had been too late.

He took her blood pressure. 'OK, that's fine, lovely and low,' he said, and turned away, busying himself with his notes to give her privacy to push her arm back into her sleeve.

'Right, long list of questions,' he said. 'Do you have any clotting or circulation difficulties?' She shook her head. 'Or any history of stroke or heart attack in the family?' Again she shook her head. 'Liver or kidney disease, epilepsy, any previous reaction to levonorgestrel, which is the active ingredient in this drug?'

She shook her head again. 'No, nothing.'

'Good. Are you on any prescriptions at the moment? Antibiotics, antifungals, anything like that?'

'No.'

'Are you taking St John's wort?'

She shook her head. 'No.'

'And you're over sixteen, this is for you and it's less than seventy-two hours since you had unprotected sex?'

She blushed again. 'Less than eighteen. It was just after midnight.'

He felt his mouth tighten. More details that he didn't need! 'That's fine. It's just that there's a time limit. OK,' he said, pulling the prescription pad towards him. 'It's a drug called Levonelle One-Step, it's a single dose, and it may either delay or advance your period. You'll need to do another pregnancy test if you haven't had a period within two weeks, but you've got the other test in the pack. Take the pill as soon as possible, and if you vomit within three hours you have to assume you've lost the pill and you'll need another dose. I also have to point out that it doesn't give protection against sexually transmitted diseases, but if you're getting one from my son I'd like to know why, and if he's getting one from you I expect he would, too.'

She blushed hotly. 'He won't get anything from me. I've only ever been with him, and he said I was his first.'

He glanced at Tom, who shifted uncomfortably and nodded. 'It's only Kel,' he agreed, and his hand slid across the table and caught her fingers, wrapping them in his hand in a comforting gesture that brought a lump to Hugh's throat.

He cleared it, suddenly feeling very old and alone. 'Right—here you go. You'd better take the money and go and sort this out—and, Kelly, I've told Tom he's to take you to the sexual health clinic and make some more appropriate arrangements for contraception. They can give you the best advice. You can't rely on this, it's a one-off. It's a very powerful drug, and I'd hate you to think you can just use it instead of taking appropriate contraceptive action.'

'Dad, we did,' Tom protested. 'I wouldn't ever be that irresponsible. It was an accident.'

'And it probably wouldn't have happened if you hadn't been drinking—go on, go and get it and sort yourselves out. I also think you need to talk to your mother, Kelly. I would imagine she knows anyway, as she was there last night—'

'She wasn't. She was away with her sister,' Kelly admitted, looking a little shamefaced. 'She thought I was staying with a friend.'

Hugh rolled his eyes and sighed. 'Kelly, tell her the truth.'

'She'll kill me!'

'No, she won't. She's your mother. She loves you. Don't shut her out, and don't lie to her. She deserves better than that.'

He watched them go, then went to find Lucy, who hopefully didn't know this last twist in the tale. She was sitting cross-legged on her bed, her television on in the background, doing her homework on her lap.

'So, have you killed him?' she asked cheerfully.

'No, I haven't killed him.'

'You told him to come home and he didn't! You would have killed me!'

'No, I wouldn't. I would have done exactly what I did with Tom—talked you to death. How was Amy?'

'Great. We watched a video.' She went on to describe it in tedious detail, but she was laughing and animated and utterly up-front, and he was delighted to hear every boring moment of the film, because it made it so obvious that she hadn't been somewhere else, getting herself into trouble.

And at the age of fourteen he really didn't need her getting herself into trouble. One at a time was more than enough.

'Are you OK if I go out for a bit?' he asked, and she tipped her head on one side and studied him curiously.

'With Eve?' she asked, seeing straight through him, and he held her frank gaze with difficulty.

'Why on earth would you think that? I just fancied a bit of fresh air. I thought I might go down to the river.'

'Yeah, right,' she said, grinning. 'Go on, go and see

your *registrar*. I'll be fine. I'm going to bed in a minute, we didn't get much sleep last night.'

He kissed the top of her head, and was just leaving the room when she added, 'She's pretty, by the way. Nice. I can see what you see in her.'

'Oh, I'm so glad you approve my choice of work colleague,' he said drily, and ran down the stairs before she could come up with anything else. He pulled on a jumper, picked up his phone and car keys and got the car out of the garage. He didn't really know where he was going, but he felt restless. He couldn't contact Eve anyway, he didn't have her number—except he did, of course, because she'd phoned him on Sunday. Heavens, was that only yesterday? So her number would be in his call register.

He dug his phone out of his pocket, nearly dropping it in his haste, and after giving himself a stern talking-to he stuck it in the hands-free cradle, tracked her number down and then hit the call button as he pulled out of the drive and headed down the street.

CHAPTER FOUR

'Eve?'

'Hugh! Hi. Everything all right?'

He chuckled. 'Sort of, in a rather chaotic way. Look, I wondered if you were doing anything?'

There was a second's silence. 'Now? Not really. I was contemplating wallowing in the bath, but I'm feeling too lazy to even do that. Why?'

He felt his gut clench at the mental image of her in the bath and crushed it immediately. 'We could go for a drink, if you're not too tired.'

Another hesitation, then she said, 'Or you could come here. You can be my first visitor. I'll even dig out a packet of crisps for you.'

'Done.' He got directions from her and pulled up outside her apartment block two minutes later. She was so close to him—walking distance. He hadn't realised. He keyed in her number on the entry-phone, and she answered, buzzed to let him in and was waiting for him when he emerged from the lift.

'Hi. Come in. Welcome to my little oasis.'

It was. Calm, tranquil, all pale neutrals and soft lighting.

It was a little soulless, a little too neutral and corporate, but just at the moment it was exactly what he needed, and so was Eve, dressed down for the evening in soft, faded jeans and a baggy sweatshirt.

'This is nice,' he said, smiling at her ruefully. 'Much better than a noisy pub. Thanks.'

'You're welcome. Have a seat. Fancy a glass of wine? I've got some white open.'

'A small one would be lovely.'

He lowered himself into the corner of the sofa, looked out at the lights sparkling on the river and sighed, feeling the tension leave him. Well, most of it.

'I owe you an apology,' he began.

'No, you don't. It was just one of those awkward things. Want to talk about it?' she asked, setting the glass down in front of him and plopping into the other corner of the sofa, one foot tucked under her bottom.

'No,' he said frankly, and realised she looked slightly relieved. 'I'm just sorry you stumbled in on it.'

'Me, too. It was a private family moment. It won't go anywhere.'

He laughed ruefully. 'I expect all the neighbours heard anyway, so it doesn't really matter, but thanks. I've sorted it out.'

She nodded. 'Handy having a dad in the business.'

'Just so long as they don't make a habit of it.' He picked up his wine, sipped it, made an appreciative noise and had another sip. 'That's lovely.'

'House-warming present from my brother. He chucked it at me as I left on Friday. I know nothing about wine except that it gives me a headache if I have too much—and that can be as little as two glasses.'

'Bit of a lightweight, are we?' he teased, and she grinned and threw a peanut at him.

'Is that for me?' he asked, fielding it and popping it in his mouth, and she pushed the bowl towards him.

'Have some—or those root vegetable crisps. They're nice.'

'I like the dark red ones—the beetroot.'

'I like them all. So do my hips. I have to ration myself to special occasions.'

He felt oddly flattered. 'Am I a special occasion?' he asked, trying not to think about her hips, and she smiled.

'It's a house-warming party, isn't it?'

'Bit quiet.'

'That's fine. Don't want to upset my neighbours in the first week.'

He laughed wryly. 'I've given up on that. Our neighbours are resigned to our presence now, I think, but we've had the odd spat. Mostly about the music.'

'Ah, yes, the teenage head-banging stuff.'

'Mmm,' he agreed, and shifted slightly, turning more towards her. 'Tell me about the professor,' he said.

'The professor?' She looked slightly startled. 'He's just a dirty old man.'

'I gathered. Did he try and hush you up?'

'I never made any noise. I just asked him not to touch me ever again. He told me not to be so prissy. I said if he stopped the nonsense, out of respect for his friendship with my father, I wouldn't do anything official, but if he touched me again, I would.'

'And he withdrew the job offer?'

She nodded. 'Just like that.'

'So what did your father think?'

Her eyes clouded. 'My father's dead, but no doubt he would have thought it was my fault.'

'Your fault?'

She shrugged. 'I shouldn't have gone into a male-dominated profession.'

'Medicine? Is it?'

'I don't think so, but he did—or thought it ought to be.'

Was there a hint of bitterness there? Possibly. 'So what did your boyfriend think?' he asked instead.

She tipped back her head and laughed softly, relaxing instantly. 'Is that a subtle way of finding out if I have a boyfriend?' she asked, and he gave her a crooked smile.

'Have you?'

'No. Have you got a wife?'

He felt his smile fade. 'No. No, I haven't got a wife. Not anymore. She died eleven years ago of an undiagnosed ectopic pregnancy that ruptured.'

Eve's dismay was evident. Her soft grey eyes widened, and her mouth parted in a small sound of distress. She shook her head slightly. 'Oh, Hugh—I'm so sorry. That must have been horrific.'

He shrugged. 'It was—but it was a long time ago.'

'Is that why you went into obstetrics?'

He shook his head. 'No. I went into obstetrics because of Tom and Lucy. Being there when they were born was so amazing, so fantastic, it was like a light switching on. Losing Jo—well, it was just coincidence that it was related to obstetrics, but I tell you what, I'm hot on ectopics now, and I make sure my staff are.'

'I bet,' Eve murmured. 'So what happened? How was it missed?'

'They thought it was appendicitis and decided to wait and see, without doing a pregnancy test, just relying on her patchy menstrual history. She ruptured and haemorrhaged, and lost consciousness. By the time they realised what was going on it was too late.'

Her brows pulled together in a troubled frown. 'Where were you?'

'At work—in the same hospital. I was on my way over to see her again, to talk to them about it. I was only a lowly house officer, but I was worried they weren't asking the right questions. Seems I was right to be worried, but I didn't say so in time.'

'And you blame yourself.'

He shrugged. 'Not entirely. I know it wasn't my responsibility but, nevertheless, my intervention might have saved her, so, yes, I blame myself.'

Eve said nothing, just stared down into her wine and gave him a moment to shift gears. He pulled himself together.

'So. No boyfriend.'

She laughed and looked up, her eyes gentle. 'No boyfriend. No complications. Just a job I never thought I'd get and a boss who seems to be turning out all right after all.'

He couldn't help but chuckle. 'Is that so? Despite the fact that you wanted to hit me last week when you came into the interview room and realised who I was?'

She coloured softly. 'Was it so obvious?'

'Only to me, but I would have felt the same. Probably would have done it—punched my lights out—and I deserved it. It was mean. I apologise. And I'll try and be a good boss in future.'

'You'll do,' she teased. 'Nobody's perfect—and you haven't groped me yet.'

No. Not for want of thinking about it, though, but she didn't need to know that, he told himself with another twinge of guilt.

'I promised,' he reminded her, and thought if he wasn't going to break his promise he'd better get himself out of there sharpish before he gave in to the temptation to lean forward, wrap his hand around the back of her neck and ease her towards him until their mouths just touched…

'I should go,' he said, wondering if it was his imagination or if his voice was really that gruff.

She didn't try and stop him, just smiled and showed him to the door. 'I'll see you in the morning,' she said cheerfully, and he nodded and took the necessary two steps out into the corridor outside.

'See you in the morning,' he echoed, and walked away from her calm, undemanding presence with a reluctant heart.

So. He was single.

So what? There was a world of difference between single and available, and she didn't need any reminding of that. She was single, but she certainly wasn't available, at least not as far as Hugh was concerned, and she didn't think he was available either.

Not if the bleak look in his eyes when he'd talked about losing Jo was anything to go by. If ever there was a man who wasn't over his late wife, he'd been sitting in her flat that evening.

Besides, even if he was available, she wasn't interested in him. She'd got her agenda all mapped out. OK, the professor had put a hiccup in it, but she'd ended up with a better job as a result, a job she would far rather have had, so she supposed in a way she should be grateful to him.

Career-wise, it had been a positive move, but personally? No. She didn't need to get involved with her boss, the father of two difficult and complicated teenagers who clearly needed a mother figure, a figure she was not in any way suited to being—no way!

No. Hugh Douglas was not on her agenda.

Ever.

Wednesday kicked off early with a ward round before the theatre list.

Eve handed Hugh notes, kept tabs on his stethoscope and studied him—and not just because he was a pleasure to look at. Watching him work was an education and a joy. He was so approachable, so easygoing and gentle and yet confident with his patients. He made them feel safe, she realised, and that was probably the most important attribute an obs and gynae surgeon could have, after the obvious requirement of technical skill.

People were scared. Women with gynae or obstetric problems were very scared, often, not just for themselves but for their potential children or the impact surgery could have on their relationships.

And they were shy. At the end of the day, this was all about their reproductive apparatus—about sex, and that was something intensely private and personal. Most people had great difficulty opening up and talking about things that bothered them in that area, but Hugh made it easy, using words they could understand without talking down to them or patronising them.

And he was gentle. Terribly gentle, and kind, and even though they were on a tight time scale, he never made his patients feel they were holding him up.

Eve was impressed.

And, being Eve, she said so.

He laughed a little self-consciously. 'I do my best. It doesn't always work. And talking of impressed, you must have hit all the right buttons with Jeannie and Paul. They've called the baby Eve.'

She felt her skin glow with delight. 'Really? Oh, how amazing. Bless them. That's never happened to me before!'

He shook his head. 'It's a good job you've got a nice name, because it's bound to happen again.' He checked his watch, frowning at it. 'Right, we'd better go and get started. The list's grown already, and we've only been on take ten minutes!'

She'd already watched him operate, last Thursday when he'd done Jeannie's section, and yesterday doing his day case list, but this time was different. These were gynae patients, women with a host of different problems, and some of them were very tricky.

Yesterday had been easy by comparison, mostly sterilisations, and he'd let her do those while he'd watched and assisted.

Now Hugh let her close after a hysterectomy for a woman with fibroids who'd been having blood transfusions since she'd been admitted on Monday, and as she tied off the last suture, he nodded and stripped off his gloves.

'Excellent. Next up is a prolapse repair—a bladder and

urethral repair following a breech delivery two years ago. She's got stress incontinence and her urethra's bulging down into her vagina, causing pain on intercourse. We need to lift it and secure her bladder to straighten the urethra. Ever done this before?'

She shook her head. 'No. I've assisted, but I'd rather see how you do it before I attempt it. I'd rather do it your way than someone else's, and I don't want to mess it up for her.'

He nodded agreement. 'Fine. Suits me. You can do the next one.'

And so it continued, taking turns so she did what she felt confident with, assisted when she didn't or if he wanted to show her a specific technique, and by the end of the morning her head was reeling but she was ecstatic. She was learning so much from him, and although it would be a long time before she felt confident she could do things his way and could take a list herself, she was happy to work under his supervision and with him assisting, especially if it wasn't too complex a case.

And the things they were doing would make so much difference to women's lives, making better the things that women never complained about but merely suffered with in silence, often for years. No. Gynae was interesting—every bit as interesting as obstetrics, she realised, and hugely satisfying, much more than she'd really expected.

As their last patient was wheeled out to Recovery, he stripped off his gloves, dumped the gown in the bin and grinned at her. 'Excellent. Between you and Oliver maybe I'll get a holiday this year after all!'

Eve laughed with a mixture of relief and concern. 'Don't go planning your escape too soon,' she cautioned, but he just chuckled and wrapped a warm, firm hand around her shoulder and squeezed.

'You'll do. You're a very welcome addition to the team. Thank you for joining us.'

Her heart swelled with pride, and her head was in danger of following suit. 'Careful, I won't get through the doorway if you keep on like that,' she teased, and his hand squeezed again and then lifted away, leaving her with a curious sense of loss.

'We'll widen it especially for your head,' he replied, then glanced at the clock. 'Right, let's go and find out what else is in store for us.'

'Are we changing?'

He shook his head. 'Only into fresh blues. There's bound to be something that's cropped up. We'll grab a sandwich in the canteen if we have time, but otherwise we'll be back up here in minutes, I can almost guarantee it.'

He wasn't wrong about them being needed, but it wasn't for Theatre, it was on the labour ward for a perfectly normal, perfectly straightforward delivery of a staff baby.

'Brilliant timing, Meg Maguire's in labour,' Molly told them as they arrived on the ward.

'Any problems?'

She shook her head. 'No—and I don't really have a job. Ben's taken over her labour and pain management, and we're on the fringes.'

Eve's curiosity was piqued. 'Is that *the* Ben Maguire? The TV guy who did the fly-on-the-wall documentary here in A and E?' she asked, and Molly nodded.

'Ex-TV guy. He's gone back to medicine. He's working here now in paediatric pain management, and he's doing all sorts of things to Meg. Shiatsu, massage, acupuncture, TENS, meditation techniques—you name it, they're doing it, and it seems to be keeping her very calm and focussed. Fantastic labour. She's progressing really well. She's in the water at the moment, and it's all candlelight and soft music and scented oils. Gorgeous. I'm taking notes for my own delivery.'

Eve blinked. 'Sounds a bit New Age,' she said doubtfully, but Molly just laughed.

'I told you I'd show you a nice, straightforward labour, didn't I? I think this one might be it. Come see.'

'Won't they mind?'

She shook her head. 'Not if we're quiet. Hugh's got to attend anyway—it's protocol for staff. One more won't make a difference, but I will check.'

They slipped through the door, and Molly went and spoke softly to them.

They lifted their heads, smiled and beckoned them over to the water pool. 'Hi, Hugh.' Meg held out her hand, and Hugh took it and squeezed gently.

'Hi, yourself. I gather you're doing really well.'

'So far. Ben's being great.'

Ben was kneeling behind her on the outside of the pool, so she lay back against his chest and he could reach her tummy to make slow, gentle circles over her bump with his hands.

'This is Eve, my new registrar,' Hugh said introducing her to them. 'I'm trying to break her in gently and show her something normal. Are you OK with us being here?'

'Sure,' she said, then a look of intense concentration came

over her face, and she dropped her head back against Ben's shoulder, turned her face towards him and moaned softly.

'Oh—it's getting stronger.'

'OK. Breathe with me, sweetheart. Nice and light, keep it soft—great, you're doing fine. Look at me, look at my eyes—that's good. Imagine you're riding a wave, going up, up, nearly there—and coming down…'

His voice was soothing and tender, his hands stroking lightly over the baby, and Meg's chest rose and fell rapidly as she panted rhythmically in time to Ben's soft chant.

Her breathing slowed again to a more normal rate, and she closed her eyes for a second. Then they flew open and she sought Molly's hand.

'Something's happening. I think I'm weeing.'

'That'll be your waters breaking. We'd better get you out now and have a look at you, OK?'

'I don't want to get out,' she protested softly, but Ben encouraged her, helped her to her feet and towelled her gently dry before helping her onto the bed.

'Let's get you out of that wet T-shirt,' Molly suggested, and Ben changed her into a dry one just in time for her next contraction.

'Ben!' Meg said frantically, and he gathered her to his chest, rocking her slowly, murmuring soothing words of comfort and encouragement. One hand was on her shoulder, the other circling slowly over the baby, and she leant on him and panted.

'I can't do it, Ben! I can't do this!' she protested at one point, but he just rocked her and stroked her and she seemed to calm.

'She's hotting up,' Molly said quietly to them, letting the

couple deal with it alone, then moving in as the contraction eased to examine Meg.

'Let's just check your progress, poppet,' Molly murmured. A few seconds later she stripped off her gloves and looked around. 'OK, you're there, Meg. You can push whenever you're ready. Where do you want to be? On the floor? On the bed? Kneeling, standing, crouching, lying over a ball?'

'Ball,' she said, struggling off the bed and starting to pant again. 'Oh, damn. Ben! You got me into this—damn well get me out of it!'

He closed his eyes and chuckled. 'OK, sweetheart. Just lie on here.'

'I want you to hold me!' she protested, pushing the ball away desperately. Turning towards him, she hooked her arms round his neck and hung on him.

'You'll make your mind up in a minute,' he teased tenderly, locking his hands together behind her back so she was supported under her armpits. 'It's OK, my darling, I've got you, you just relax now and do what Molly tells you.'

'I've got to push!' she screamed, and Molly just rubbed her lower back firmly and told her to go ahead.

'Deep breath and push down but keep your mouth open—that's lovely. The baby's crowning now. The next push should do it. Nice and steady.'

'I can feel her,' she said, freeing Ben's neck with one hand and reaching down to touch her baby's head with incredulous fingers. 'Oh, Ben, I can feel her hair!'

The look of wonder on her face brought tears to Eve's eyes, and it dawned on her that there was no way she'd get through this delivery without crying her eyes out.

And then she found her hand wrapped firmly in a strong, comforting grip, and she gripped back, her concentration intense as she watched Meg give birth to their beautiful, perfect little daughter.

Ben lowered her carefully to the sterile sheets, kneeling behind her to support her as Molly put the baby to Meg's breast.

'Hello, little one,' he said unevenly, his hand lying over the baby in Meg's arms, and Eve realised they were all in tears.

Ben, Meg, Molly—and even Hugh's eyes were suspiciously bright.

'Congratulations,' he said quietly, then, still holding Eve firmly by the hand, he led her out of the birthing suite and into a nearby office, kicked the door shut and pulled her into his arms.

'OK now?' he asked after a minute, and she sniffed and laughed and released her death grip on his ribcage.

'Fine. Sorry. It's just…'

'A miracle. I know. And it doesn't get any better. It still gets me every time.'

He stood back, taking her shoulders in his hands and looking down at her with an indulgent and curiously tender smile.

'Are you really all right?'

She nodded, sniffing again and hunting fruitlessly for a tissue.

He handed her one from the box on the desk, gave her another just in case and, looping an arm carelessly round her shoulders, steered her towards the door.

'Come on, let's grab a late lunch before all hell breaks loose, because it will, you know. It always does.'

And he opened the door, ushered her down the corridor to the lift, then along to the canteen and bought her lunch.

It occurred to her that this was the third time since the day of the interview, less than a week ago, that he'd fed her in one way or another, and it was about time she did something about it.

'I owe you a meal,' she said through a mouthful of sandwich.

'Why?'

'Because you keep feeding me.'

'Self-interest,' he said with a chuckle. 'I just want to keep you functioning efficiently so I can plan my holiday.'

Was that really a flicker of disappointment she felt? How silly. She didn't want complications! 'What will you do with the kids when you go away?' she asked, casting about for a safe topic. 'Take them with you?'

He groaned. 'Don't. I can't bear to think about it. Lucy's only fourteen—I can't really leave her, but I can't see Tom wanting to come without Kelly, and I'm damned if I need the two of them canoodling in the wings while Lucy and I sit about like gooseberries and make small talk! So either I leave them at home and goodness knows what'll happen, or I take the grandparents with me and spend a week with my parents or in-laws. Heads they win, tails I lose. Nightmare.'

Eve laughed without humour, the image too awful to contemplate. No, she definitely didn't want complications, particularly not complications like that!

'I wonder if Ben and Meg have any idea what's in store?' she murmured, and Hugh groaned.

'I hope not, for their sake. They might as well have a

modicum of emotional peace while the going's good. Believe me, it won't last.'

No, it certainly wouldn't. She tipped her head on one side. 'You must have been very young when you had Tom.'

'Seventeen,' he said quietly. 'That's why I freaked out last night. History repeating itself. I just saw my life all over again, and it wasn't what I wanted for him and Kelly. It wasn't what I wanted for me and Jo, either, but the morning-after pill wasn't available when we were kids, and we just got on with it. It helped that we loved each other to bits, and our parents were all fantastic about it and took so much of the pressure off us.'

'They must have done for you to go to university.'

'We both did,' he told her, to her surprise. 'Jo finished her A levels just before Tom was born, and she managed to switch her course to a less demanding one, but still in Nottingham, so we were together. Her father got transferred there and we got a house between us. Her mother looked after Tom during the week, and at weekends they went home to their own house in Bury St Edmunds and left us to be parents. And it was great.'

'But you were so young.'

He shrugged. 'Yeah, but we were happy, and Tom was such a good baby. Then when we were twenty-one she had Lucy, just after the end of her course, and it was easier then for a while, because she was at home looking after the children while I was at college. And then two years after that she got pregnant again and—well, you know the rest.'

How incredibly sad. Eve shook her head slowly. 'I'm sorry—I didn't mean to drag it all up again,' she murmured, feeling guilty, but Hugh just smiled at her and shook his head.

'Don't worry, Eve. It was years ago. I'll never stop being frustrated by the waste of her life, but I've let her go now. I'm just left dealing with the aftermath of our teenage hormones, and that gets more complicated the older they get.'

His smile was wry, and she smiled back with feeling.

'So it would seem. I have to say you're welcome to family life—much too messy for me.'

'Tell me about it,' he said with a bleak chuckle. 'More tea?'

But their patients had other ideas. His bleep went, followed rapidly by hers, and while he went up to the ward to see one of their post-op patients, she went to A and E to assess Mrs Ryan, a pregnant woman who'd been involved in a low-speed collision outside her son's playgroup.

Her toddler was wriggling and squirming in a nurse's arms, refusing to be entertained or distracted by toys. After checking her over thoroughly, Eve could find no obstetric reason to detain Mrs Ryan, who was anxious to go.

'Just promise you'll come straight back in if you have the slightest concern,' Eve said, doubt nagging at the back of her mind even though the portable ultrasound had picked up nothing and Mrs Ryan's obs were all normal. 'Any pain, bleeding, leaking fluid, a show—anything that might indicate you're starting your labour early or that something's wrong. But hopefully you'll be fine and you'll continue to term without any problems.'

'You look worried,' the senior sister, Angie, said to her as they left the cubicle together a few moments later.

'I don't know,' Eve said, shaking her head. 'Not worried, exactly…'

'Just not certain?'

Eve nodded. 'Something like that.'

Angie shrugged. 'We all do it—get funny feelings. I'll check her again before I let her go. So—how are Meg and Ben and the baby?'

'Oh—you know them?'

'Oh, yes. Meg's one of ours. They met when Ben was filming here. Love at first sight and all that. I've never seen anyone fall so quick—well, apart from Fliss and Tom. There must be something in the water down here!' She chuckled. 'Anyway, how are they all?'

Eve remembered the looks on their faces, and smiled. 'They're great. The baby's gorgeous—absolutely lovely. Perfect. Ten tiny fingers, ten tiny toes, Ben's mouth, Meg's nose—I don't know. Beautiful. Somehow it makes everything fall into place.'

'And Meg?'

'She's fine. They're all fine,' she said. 'It was a beautiful, peaceful textbook delivery, and it was a privilege to be there. I felt really honoured—does that sound stupid?'

Angie shook her head. 'No. I know exactly what you mean. Give them my love when you see them. Tell them I'll be up when I can. And if you like I'll keep Mrs Ryan in for a while, keep an eye on her for you. Would that be an idea?'

Eve nodded, relieved. 'Can you do that? Will she stay? I don't want to admit her, really, I'm just—'

'Not certain. That's fine. I'll dream up some excuse and delay her for a while and keep an eye. We'll be in touch.'

'Thanks.'

She went back up to the ward and found Hugh cuddling the Maguire baby.

'Angie sends her love,' Eve told the proud parents, and

then turned to Hugh. 'There's a patient down there—a Mrs Ryan. She's had a low-speed RTA, and she's fine. Thirty-five weeks.'

'But?'

She shrugged. 'I don't know. I couldn't find anything wrong, but I just have a gut feeling.'

'Act on it. Admit her if you're uncertain.'

'But there's nothing wrong.'

'There often isn't. We've got space—I'd rather be safe than sorry.'

'Angie's sitting on her for now. She'll let us know if there's anything. Anyway, she's got a toddler, she won't want to leave him just because I've got a hunch.'

'Don't worry about it. I'll get the ward on standby for her.'

Eve was startled. 'Really? But it's probably nothing—just me being over-cautious.'

'Don't knock it. Listen to your instincts.'

Heavens. Everyone was telling her to listen to her instincts. She just hoped they were reliable and weren't going to turn her into a laughing stock. She didn't like it one bit, but there had just been something…

When Mrs Ryan's pressure crashed suddenly two hours later and she was rushed into Theatre for an emergency section because of a placental abruption, Eve heaved a sigh of relief and conceded privately that maybe—just maybe—there was a place in medicine for gut feelings.

Or maybe there had been something that she'd recognised subconsciously as a warning sign but just hadn't catalogued.

Yes. That had to be it. Nothing to do with guts.

At all.

CHAPTER FIVE

'GOOD call,' Hugh said when it was over. 'So, was there really nothing to go on? Did she have any symptoms at all?'

Eve shook her head. 'No, nothing—and nothing showed on the ultrasound. It just felt…wrong.'

'You must be fey,' he teased, but she got the feeling he was impressed. She wasn't, because it had been such an odd sensation, and, no matter how she'd tried to justify it to herself, there wasn't anything else she could put it down to, just a gut feeling that not all was quite as it seemed, and she didn't want to work like that. She wanted facts and figures, things she could quantify, not fey nonsense. That was too scary, too intuitive, and it might let her down.

'Hey, stop fretting. We all do this from time to time. It doesn't make you weird, it just makes you a good doctor. Relax. Chill. Live with it.'

His eyes were kind, his mouth quirking into a smile that did silly things to her insides, and she got the strangest feeling he was going to hug her.

Again.

For the second time today.

Uh-uh. There was only so much hugging a person could

cope with and still fool herself she could keep things professional, so she moved out of his way, giving them both a little more room, and flashed him a smile.

'Consider me chilled,' she said. 'Right. I'm going to grab a break before I go and check on the post-ops. I haven't had a drink for hours.'

'Good idea. I'll join you,' he said promptly.

So much for putting space between them, but it seemed it was only her head that was objecting, because her body fell neatly into step beside him as he headed for the lift that would take them down to the entry level and the little café at the back of the hospital that the public still hadn't really tracked down.

He picked up a mug of tea and a chocolate-chip muffin, and she went for coffee and an iced bun, beating him to the checkout and paying for both lots before he could get his wallet out of his pocket.

He frowned at her, but she just shook her head. 'Uh-uh. My turn. I owe you loads of meals, and at this rate I'll end up having to cook you a slap-up dinner to make up for it.'

Something wistful flickered in his eyes for a second. 'Sounds good,' he murmured. 'It's years since a woman under fifty cooked for me. When did you have in mind?'

She laughed a little awkwardly. 'I haven't asked you yet.'

'Well, feel free. I'm not busy on Friday night, and you aren't either.'

'You sound very sure.'

'I am. I checked the rota this morning.'

'Why?'

His grin was wry. 'Because I was going to ask you out to dinner. However, if I've got a better offer…'

Eve felt her heart thump against her ribs. This was so silly. He was her boss. She had to keep a distance—not lure him into her very cosy apartment and threaten the status quo. A glass of wine and a packet of crisps had been dangerous enough. Maybe dinner out would be safer. More people, less intimate.

Further from a nice, big, comfy double bed.

'No better offer. Feel free to ask me,' she retorted, and he laughed and sat back.

'I rather liked the sound of you cooking for me,' he said softly, his eyes tracking over hers, the warmth in them unmistakable now.

She shook her head. 'Not enough credit yet.'

His grin was lazy and easy, but the heat in his eyes was anything but. 'I'll have to do something about that—something really special that'll crank up the balance and tip the scales.' He drained his cup, brushed off his hands and met her eyes again. 'Seven-thirty, Friday night. Smart-casual. I'll pick you up.'

And without waiting for her to reply, he got up and walked away, leaving her struggling for breath and common sense. Just then she didn't seem to have enough of either!

He must be mad, Hugh thought on his way into the hospital on Friday morning. He had to work with her, and muddying the waters was just crazy. So was he—driven crazy by the prospect of spending an entire evening with her in a romantic little bistro just designed for lovers.

'How's it going?'

He turned to find Julia falling into step beside him, and his heart sank. The last thing he needed was the clinical director of their department interrogating him on his new staff member.

'It's going fine,' he said. 'She's excellent.'

'Good. I'm glad. I'd hate you to be proved wrong at a patient's expense. Just remember—keep your hands to yourself. Which reminds me, there's a resuscitation refresher course running tonight. I've checked the rota and you're free, so I've booked you in.'

'That doesn't mean I'm available,' he pointed out, but she just raised an eyebrow.

'Unless it's life or death, you're free,' she said bluntly. 'This is a very important course and I think we should take advantage of it. Besides, I've booked you a place.'

'OK. You'd better book us all in, then.'

Her brows hitched together into a frown. 'All?'

'Mmm,' he said, suppressing his smile. 'Me, Oliver and Eve. Alison will be fine, she's just done a stint in A and E.'

Her frown deepened. 'I don't know if we can fit all of you in.'

'Sure you can. We'll take turns, be the same person, if necessary.'

'Oh.' She looked disappointed—no, make that thwarted—and his suspicions were confirmed with her next breath. 'I had thought we could get together afterwards—have a chat about things over a drink.'

Hell, would she never give up? 'Sorry, I've got plans for later.'

Involving Eve, and a postponement of their dinner date, but Julia didn't need to know that. In fact, the less she knew about his private life, especially where it overlapped with his new registrar's, the better.

'Cancel them.'

He shook his head. 'Sorry, no can do. Carved in stone.'

'Family?'

'You guessed,' he said, failing to point out that she'd guessed wrong. 'Sorry, got to fly, I've got paperwork to catch up on and we're still on take, so any minute now I'll be needed in Theatre. Don't forget, three of us, please.'

And for the second time in a few minutes, he walked away from a woman without giving her a chance to argue.

'Change of plan.'

Eve tilted her head and felt her brows quirk together. 'Plan?'

'For tonight. Julia thought we should do a resus refresher course. She's booked us in—you, me and Oliver. Six-thirty in the teaching block.'

'Oh.' How ridiculous, to feel such a surge of disappointment when she'd been panicking about their date anyway and wondering why she'd agreed! 'We'll have to take a rain-check on dinner,' she said, hoping she didn't sound as pathetically forlorn as she felt, but Hugh shook his head.

'Only for a couple of hours. Unless you're going to turn into a pumpkin or something, we can make it later. I've made the reservation for nine-thirty to be on safe side. That should still give you time to get all gussied up if we finish by seven-thirty.'

'*That* gussied up?' she said on a splutter of laughter. 'Where on earth are you taking me?'

'Somewhere nice,' he said softly. 'Somewhere to spoil us both a bit.'

Her heart thumped against her ribs, but she ignored

the warning. 'Nine-thirty? I can get as gussied as I get in ten minutes. Should we make it earlier so we don't starve to death?'

He grinned. 'I'll make it eight forty-five. We don't want you fading away.'

She grinned back. 'Sounds good. And I thought it was the coach that turned into a pumpkin.'

His shrug was the sexiest thing she'd seen in ages, and she had to swallow her little moan of appreciation. 'Whatever,' he said, his grin still teasing around those gorgeous honey-brown eyes. 'Right. Ward round. I've got mums that need inducing and patients for discharge and I think there's a tricky delivery under way, if Molly's harassed look is anything to go by.'

'Tricky?' she said, falling in beside him as he set off down the ward, notes in hand.

'Mmm. A breech that's failed to co-operate, wouldn't turn and is working on getting stuck. I think if there's no progress soon, she'll be in Theatre.'

'What a shame.'

'It is, but not as much of a shame as losing a perfectly healthy baby, which might be the alternative.'

He paused beside a bed, squirted gel on his hands and rubbed it in as he greeted their first patient, Beth Ryan, the woman who'd had the placental abruption on Wednesday.

'Mrs Ryan, good to see you. How are you feeling?' he asked, and she rolled her eyes.

'Apart from having an abdominal incision I wasn't reckoning on, a fractious two-year-old who's driving my husband crazy and a car with a hole in the side of it? Oh, I'm peachy!'

'But you're alive, and so's your baby, thanks to Eve here and her gut feelings, so it isn't all bad,' Hugh reminded her gently, and her eyes softened as she glanced at the crib beside her.

'Yes. We're alive, and you're right, that's all that matters. So I have you to thank for not letting me go home?' she added, smiling at Eve, who nodded.

'Well, sort of. Mr Douglas agreed that it was better to be safe than sorry if I had any doubts.'

'Eve doesn't like gut feelings,' Hugh put in, 'but sometimes they come up trumps.' He smiled at her and turned his attention to the baby for a moment. 'So how is young baby Ryan?'

'Greedy and doing really well. They kept him in SCBU for the first night, but they said at thirty-five weeks he was pretty much ready anyway, and as he's feeding so well, they thought he should be here with me. I'm not going to argue, I hated it up there. All those instruments and everybody hovering and looking haggard and sick with fright—it scared me to bits.'

'It can be pretty grim up there, but they have the most incredible success stories.'

'Oh, I know, and if he'd needed it I would have been more than grateful. I'm just even more grateful that he didn't, if you know what I mean.'

'Absolutely. Right, let's have a look at your tummy and make sure it's healing OK, and then, if you're feeling all right over the weekend and they're happy for you to take the baby home, you can go home on Monday.'

She looked worried, but Hugh didn't see, his head bent over her abdomen, checking her suture line and the height of her fundus to make sure her uterus was shrinking back down nicely.

Eve, though, watching her, wondered if she was uneasy about going home so soon. 'Is that a problem, going home on Monday?' she asked softly, and Beth shrugged.

'Not really. I just feel—I don't know. A bit nervous. Christopher's a bit full on, you know? Toddlers can be like loose cannons, and I'm quite sore. I don't know if I can look after him yet.'

'No, you can't,' Hugh said firmly, perching on the arm of the chair and looking sternly at her. 'Definitely. You have to have help. You can look after the baby, but the two-year-old is too heavy for you to lift. You can cuddle him and read to him and play with his toys when the baby's asleep, but someone else will have to do the physical stuff for a while—maybe weeks. If you aren't careful you could end up splitting your stitches and getting an incisional hernia.'

'Oh.' She sagged back against the pillows, her eyes troubled, but then she shrugged. 'Oh, well, if it has to be, it has to be. My mother's offered to come, but I didn't like to ask her. I should be able to cope.'

'No, ask her,' Hugh advised. 'You'll need her and, in my experience, being needed is what mothers do best. I'll see you in my follow-up clinic in a few weeks just to make sure everything's as it ought to be, but I'm sure it will be. Until then, you take care, and you'll be surprised how much better you feel by Monday, anyway.'

They left her phoning her husband on the patient-line phone attached to the bedside TV screen, and as they walked away, they heard her say, 'Do you want the good news first, or the bad news?'

Hugh chuckled. 'I guess mother-in-law is the bad news,' he murmured, and Eve shot him a sideways look.

'I thought your mother-in-law was wonderful?'

He looked surprised. 'Oh, she is—she was fantastic when we had the children, and she's fantastic now. But I've also learned how to deal with her over the years, and we get on really well. Not everyone's that lucky. Besides, what could she find fault with in me?'

His eyes were wide and innocent, and Eve snorted. 'Apart from the things you got up to with her daughter at the tender age of seventeen—'

'Sixteen,' he corrected with a grin. 'Jo was sixteen when we met. Seventeen when Tom was conceived, eighteen when he was born—and we were married by then, so we were sort of forgiven.'

So it hadn't been a silly little teenage mistake, then, more the unfortunate consequence of a slip-up during a long-term relationship. A relationship that, without Jo's death, would probably still be going on now.

And she was having dinner tonight with Jo's husband.

A sudden shiver ran through her, and Hugh gave her a quizzical look. 'You OK?'

'I'm fine,' she said, summoning a smile. Just a trifle haunted by your late wife, she could have added, but getting that out of her would have been harder than pulling teeth.

'I wonder how Molly's delivery's going?' he murmured, and Eve was hugely relieved at the change of subject.

'Should we check?'

'Good idea.'

Eve paused. 'I've never seen a vaginal breech delivery,

only a section. Before we go in, can you tell me what your criteria are for intervening?'

'Of course. Maternal or foetal distress, mainly. Parity's a good indicator, often. Being a first baby tends to indicate a likely problem for the following head, because it's bigger than the baby's bottom so there's going to be a delay while the cervix dilates further, and in that time the cord's trapped against the baby's skull and the oxygen supply is cut off.'

'Not good.'

'No, not good. It's less of a problem in a multiparous woman because the path's already been cleared. It's a bit like trail-blazing. Once it's been done, it's usually easier for subsequent deliveries, because the tissues have been stretched, and also there tends to be less maternal tension and conflict with the process. First-time mums can be their own worst enemies without realising it, and a breech presentation just makes it worse. For that reason we almost always prefer to deliver breech-first babies by elective Caesarean section.'

'So when do you pull the plug with a multiparous woman?'

He shrugged. 'Depends. I rely on gut feeling and the instincts of the midwife.'

'Guts again,' she muttered under her breath, and Hugh laughed softly.

'Sorry. You hate it, don't you? Anything you can't find in a textbook.'

'It's just not quantifiable.'

'No. Much of life isn't. If you'd asked me at seventeen if I wanted to be a father, I would have said no. Ask me now, and, hell though they are, I couldn't begin to imagine life without my kids. It's like love. You can't measure it, or define it, but you know when it's there. And you know when it isn't.'

He paused outside the delivery room, washed his hands, gelled them and shouldered open the door a crack.

'OK to come in?'

'Hugh, sure. I was just about to bleep you. Annabel's getting rather tired but things are going OK. I'd just like you to check her, make sure you're happy.'

He pushed the door open and Eve followed him, rubbing the last of the spirit gel into her hands.

'Hi, there,' he said, going over to Annabel and placing a gentle hand on her shoulder. 'Remember me? Hugh Douglas.'

'Of course I remember you. You told me you'd make sure I was all right. I hope you meant it.'

'That's why I'm here,' he said calmly. 'How's it going? Molly says you're getting tired but it's going well.'

'I'm just exhausted. It seems to be going on much longer than my first. I never knew it would be like this.'

'It's probably slow because the baby's bottom doesn't do as good a job of dilating the cervix as the head does, so it can sometimes drag a bit. Have you considered an epidural?'

Her partner, perched on the bed beside the pillows, shook his head. 'She wants a natural delivery. It was supposed to be a home birth this time.'

'Well, to be fair, I think you have to allow her to decide now that things are changing,' he said quietly. 'A natural delivery is a lovely idea, but it isn't always possible, and at the end of the day it's the health of the mother and baby that matters.'

It was the gentlest reprimand, but Annabel's partner

Andy coloured a little, sucked in a breath, looked away and then looked back and nodded, his eyes contrite. 'Of course. I'm sorry. I wasn't being obstructive, I was just trying to fight her corner, but I don't know where it is any more.'

'Don't worry, we're onto it.'

'Will it help?' Annabel asked worriedly. 'An epidural?'

'Usually. It'll certainly ease the pain, help to relax you so you aren't fighting it, and if we need to proceed to Theatre you'll be ready to go instantly. But before I can make any decisions I need to have a look at you and assess what's going on.'

He turned to Molly. 'Can you fill us in on the case for Eve's benefit?'

'Sure. She's had X-ray pelvimetry a week ago, and there's no evidence of cephalopelvic disproportion and she's well dilated. The baby isn't big, there isn't a placenta previa and so far the cord hasn't prolapsed. Progress has been nice and steady.'

'How many weeks gestation?'

'Thirty-nine.'

Hugh nodded and snapped on a pair of gloves. 'Get gloved up, Eve, and see if you can feel what we're talking about.'

She did so, watching meanwhile as Hugh carefully examined Annabel, pressing down on her abdomen to push the baby down into the birth canal.

'OK, there doesn't seem to be any reason why that won't work. Molly, can you whistle up an anaesthetist for an epidural, please? Annabel, are you happy for Eve to examine you? She's my new registrar and she'll be assisting me in Theatre if we need to change plans, so I'd like her to know what's going on.'

'Of course,' Annabel said, nodding, but then a contraction came, and she rolled towards Andy, moaning softly.

'Just breathe nice and light,' Hugh said. 'Don't tense up, just pant lightly with your mouth open.'

'I want to push,' she said desperately, but he shook his head.

'Not just yet. Give us a few minutes if you can, there's a good girl.'

'Why the delay?' Eve asked quietly, while Annabel concentrated on panting and not pushing.

Hugh's eyes were on the foetal heart monitor as he replied. 'Because I want her cervix as effaced as possible, and there's still a little posterior lip around the back of the baby's bottom. Once that's gone, she can push like hell, but bottoms don't dilate the cervix like heads do, so I want the best possible chance. The longer she can hang on, the better.'

'OK, makes sense. Is the baby coping?'

'At the moment. All right now?' he asked as the exhausted mother sagged against the pillows, her eyes closed.

'Mmm,' she mumbled.

'Right. Eve, see if you can feel a little rim of cervix at the back, high up, or if the baby's descending now. I'll press down to bring it into reach, then let you do it.'

She slipped her fingers past the baby's little bottom, feeling for a band of muscular tissue around its back, but there was nothing.

'I can't feel it.'

'I think it's probably gone, then. That's good. I think we'll let Molly give it a go.'

But it wasn't to be that easy. The baby's body was delivered easily, but despite Annabel's massive efforts, with

Molly encouraging her and Andy supporting her body while she tried to kneel and let gravity help, the baby's heartbeat suddenly dropped to seventy with a contraction and stayed there.

Hugh watched the monitor, gave it ten seconds to recover after the contraction and shook his head.

'Sorry, Annabel, your baby's distressed and I can't leave you any longer. I'm going to have to use forceps to get her out fast.'

And he was fast. Fast, neat, efficient and within moments, it seemed, the baby was born and the neonatal team were dealing with her.

'She's a little flat—Apgar score six—but she's pinking up nicely. Come on, little one.'

Right on cue, she let out a feeble wail, took a trembling breath and bellowed.

'I never thought I'd be so pleased to hear a baby cry,' Andy said, tears streaming down his cheeks, and Annabel was laughing and crying and desperately trying to see her little daughter.

'OK, she's fine,' Josh Lancaster, the paediatrician, said with a broad grin. 'Here—your little bundle of joy, I think.'

And he laid the baby, still screaming indignantly and covered in blood and vernix, nature's very own moisturiser, on her mother's soft, warm abdomen.

'Oh, baby,' Annabel said reverently, and, reaching out her hands, cradled the tiny body to her breast.

'Let me help you,' Molly said. Turning the baby's head, she latched her onto the nipple with ease of practice, and the room descended into a blissful silence, broken only by the sound of her ferocious suckling.

'Not much wrong with that,' Josh said with satisfaction, and clapped Hugh on the shoulder. 'Nice work. See you.'

'Thanks. Didn't we do well? I reckon Molly deserves a rest, and I've done the cavalry thing. Eve? Your turn. Fancy doing some needlework?'

So for her sins Eve spent the next half-hour carefully repairing the episiotomy incision that Hugh had made to facilitate the baby's delivery, while Molly gave her step-by-step instructions on what kind of suture she liked to use for each layer and why.

'Lovely job,' Hugh said over her shoulder, popping in a few minutes into the repair. 'That should heal really well. Come and find me when you've finished, I've got something for you to do.'

The something turned out to be another cup of coffee, but by the time Eve had finished her suturing she was more than ready for it.

It was her last chance for a break for the rest of that day, but she wasn't alone. Molly, having finished the delivery Hugh had been called to assist with, then ended up taking a group of mums and tots around the maternity unit.

Eve, bumping into her while she was checking one of the post-ops, found her trailing her little brood like the Pied Piper, and couldn't help grinning.

'Looks fun,' she remarked, and Molly rolled her eyes.

'Great fun,' she said. 'It's one of our toddler parties. It helps the older siblings understand what's going on a little, and takes some of the strangeness away when they come to visit Mum and the baby. I must admit, though,' she said in a quiet aside, 'I could do without it today. I've been on my feet since eight.'

Eve looked at her more closely. 'Are you OK?'

She nodded. 'I'm fine. It's now my last day today, and I have to say, I'm glad. I had another ultrasound earlier, and Hugh thinks my dates are wrong, so I've brought my maternity leave forward a week. It seems I'm more likely to be thirty-eight weeks, not thirty-five, and I think I've worked late enough into this pregnancy if that's the case!' She turned back to the little group behind her who'd all caught up now. 'OK. Who wants a ride on one of the beds?'

Eve shook her head in disbelief at Molly's cheerful tone and left her to it. She was exhausted already and, unlike Molly, she wasn't even slightly pregnant! But she still had the resus refresher course to get through—and then, if she could stay awake long enough to do it justice, Hugh was taking her out to dinner.

Suddenly she didn't feel so tired any more.

'Wow. Amazing what you can forget.'

'Isn't it?' Eve agreed, turning to Hugh as they left the resus course a minute after eight. 'It's not that long since I was in A and E, but it seems light years away.'

He grunted. 'Tell me about it! It's years longer since I was there. Julia was right, we needed that refresher. I thought I could still intubate. Apparently not.'

'You got it on the second try,' she reminded him. 'That's pretty good.'

He grunted again. 'Not good enough. We shouldn't allow skills like that to fade, and I'm going to make sure we don't in the future. But in the immediate future—'

'I need to go home and shower and change, and so do

you,' she completed for him. 'I'll see you as soon as you're ready. Do you want me to meet you there to save time?'

He shook his head. 'It's just near you. I'll pick you up on the way. Go on, you're wasting time. Go and get gorgeous.'

Eve laughed. 'Gorgeous? I don't have that long,' she said, but he just looked at her, his eyes stroking over her like a lover's fingers.

'You've got more than enough,' he murmured, and pushed her gently towards the door. 'Go on, go. I'll see you shortly.'

She went, feeling the caress of his eyes all the way home, through every touch of the soap on her skin, the slither of her skirt as she eased it over her head—all of it, every touch, she felt as if it was his.

She realised without doubt that she wanted it to be, and if she'd had the slightest lick of sense she'd have run screaming.

CHAPTER SIX

HE PRESSED the doorbell without any real hope that Eve would be ready, but she answered the intercom instantly.

'I'll be down in a moment,' she said, and sure enough she appeared in the hallway only seconds later, dressed in a floaty, flirty skirt and a pretty top that clung in all the right places and did terrible things to his resolve. And she was wearing ridiculously high heels, ankle-breakingly high that made her legs go on for ever…

'Gorgeous enough?' she asked teasingly, doing a twirl so he could see her, and he nodded, his tie almost strangling him and his tongue so huge he was in danger of choking on it.

'Absolutely,' he said, wanting to make a teasing remark but finding his wit deserting him in favour of truth.

For a moment she looked startled, then she smiled, soft colour touching her cheeks.

'Thank you,' she said, then glanced at her watch. 'It's nearly half past. We'll be late.'

Hugh took her coat from her, holding it out so she could put it on. 'No, we won't, it's only round the corner. Can you walk in those crazy shoes or do you want to take the car?'

She laughed softly. 'I'm a woman. I can walk in anything.'

They fell into step, her long legs keeping up with his easily if he shortened his stride just a little, and amazingly he ushered her through the door of the little bistro early.

'Oh, how lovely. It's smaller than I was expecting—cosy,' she murmured, looking around, her lively and curious eyes taking it all in.

'I like it,' he replied, and smiled at the *maître d'* who appeared at his elbow. 'Hugh Douglas—reservation for eight forty-five.'

'Of course. Your table's ready for you, Mr Douglas, if you could come this way?'

He took their coats and seated them next to the window overlooking a floodlit courtyard. Immediately a jug of iced water appeared at the table, followed by a basket of bread, a bowl of oil and some marinated olives to nibble on while they contemplated the menu.

'Any recommendations?' she asked, but Hugh just shook his head.

'I've eaten here a few times, and nothing's ever missed the mark. I think you're safe whatever you choose.'

'So what are you having?'

He studied Eve. He knew quite well what he wanted, but unfortunately she wasn't on the menu. He tried to concentrate on food but, with her looking so gorgeous, it wasn't easy.

'How hungry are you?' he asked. 'Are you a pudding person, or a savoury person, or a finicky little eater?'

She laughed. 'Not finicky. Never that. I'm starving. I could manage three courses, unless they're too huge. I guess I'm an everything person.'

He felt his mouth kick up in reply to her smile. 'Me, too.

Let's go for a starter and main course and see if we've got room for the desserts. I reckon we've earned it.' He dragged his eyes off her smile, studied the menu for a moment and snapped it shut. 'Anything take your fancy?' he asked, and she looked up and met his eyes, her own rueful.

'Most of it. Deciding what to leave out's the hardest bit.'

He laughed. 'You're going to eat it, not marry it,' he reminded her, and she chuckled and shut the menu.

'You're right. I'll have what you're having.'

'The mussels and the venison?'

She scrunched up her face. 'Mussels? All that grit and garlic—yuck.'

She gave an exaggerated shudder, and he felt the laughter bubbling in his chest. 'You don't have to follow my lead. What about the *pâté* with onion marmalade? And the sea bass is wonderful here. It's wild, not farmed.'

She handed him her menu, picked up a little slice of French stick and tore it up, dipping it in the oil and popping it in her mouth. Desire hit him like a freight train. 'Sounds great,' she mumbled round the bread. 'Like I said, I could eat it all, but sadly not all on one night.'

'We'll have to come again, then,' he said, and she looked up, eyes laughing.

'I'll be the size of a house.'

'So eat lettuce in between,' he said, catching the waiter's eye.

'Ready to order, sir?'

'I think so.' He ordered the *pâté* and sea bass for Eve, then abandoned the mussels in favour of something that wasn't calculated to give him killer garlic breath. Just in case.

'Any wine, sir?'

He cocked an eyebrow at Eve. 'Wine?'

She shrugged. 'Whatever. I only want one glass. I'm a lightweight, remember?'

And he was driving, so he ordered two glasses, a red for him and a white for her, and settled back to watch her indulge her senses.

Amazing. He'd never seen anybody eat with such sheer delight. There was nothing greedy or over-indulgent in the way she tackled her food, just a single-minded dedication to the art of the chef, and no chef could fail to be flattered by her response.

They shared a dessert, though, neither of them quite up to the challenge of a whole one, but in fact he only had a couple of dips into the gloriously soft and astonishingly chocolate tart before he gave up and just settled back to watch her.

It was one of the most erotic experiences of his life.

The expression of bliss on her face was enough to drive him crazy, but then she picked up the fanned strawberry by the stalk and bit it off with her teeth, and he thought he was going to disgrace himself. Hell's teeth, she was going to kill him if she went on like this…

'Oh, wow, that was fabulous,' she said, finally setting down her dessert spoon with a look of regret.

'Sure you've finished?' he teased, eyeing her scraped plate with a smile nudging at his mouth.

She gave a rueful chuckle and chased the last taste of chocolate from her lips with the tip of her tongue, sending heat crashing through him all over again. 'Sorry,' she said with a contented smile. 'I've been a complete pig, haven't I?'

He shook his head slowly, wondering how on earth he

was going to keep his hands to himself while he walked her home. 'Not at all,' he said, wondering if his voice sounded in any way normal. 'You've done it justice. What more could anyone ask for?'

'Dignity,' she said with a self-deprecating laugh. 'Still, I've got an excuse. I've hardly eaten all week, except when you've dragged me to the canteen. I've been too busy, and today's been no exception. The last thing I had was a biscuit at eleven-thirty.'

'We'll have to make sure that doesn't happen again, then,' he said, and wondered how he could engineer feeding her every night for the next year.

Should she invite him in?

It seemed silly not to, but they'd just had coffee at the bistro, and it was such a short walk that even he couldn't need coffee again yet, so there was only one reason she'd ask him inside, and that was a lousy idea.

Her mind and her mouth seemed disconnected, though, as usual, and without thinking she turned to him at the outer door, her mouth open to issue the invitation, but before she could speak he laid a finger on her lips and shook his head.

'Don't ask me in, Eve,' he murmured, and she wondered how he could read her mind so easily. Was she so transparent, so desperate for his touch that it was written all over her face?

Probably.

'Maybe I wasn't going to,' she said, knowing he wouldn't believe her but giving it a go anyway. 'Maybe I was going to tell you I'd see you on Monday.'

His mouth kicked up in a knowing grin. 'Of course you

were.' Then the grin faded, and he dropped his hand away from her face and stepped back, his eyes suddenly intense. 'Thank you for a lovely evening.'

'Isn't that my line?'

He shook his head. 'I don't think so. Sleep well. Have a good weekend.'

And without touching her again, without a peck on the cheek or a touch of his hand or the brush of his fingers against hers, he turned on his heel and strode swiftly to his car, sliding behind the wheel and driving away without a second look.

She felt bereft.

Stupid. Stupid, stupid, stupid.

'Stupid,' she repeated out loud. 'You've got to work with him. You don't *want* him kissing you.'

Oh, yes I do, her body screamed, so loud she was sure the couple strolling along the pavement behind her just the other side of the railings would hear.

'You're mad,' she told herself firmly.

They lifted their heads and gave her a curious look, and she pretended she was talking into the intercom.

'Truly mad.'

She had a ridiculous urge to giggle, but the next few seconds of frantic searching dispatched it.

She had no keys.

She closed her eyes and groaned. She could see them clearly, on the hall table where she'd thrown them on her way in. Where she always threw them. So what now? Call a locksmith? Wait for the morning and contact the landlord? And sleep where? She couldn't even get into her car!

'Oh, damn,' she muttered, and then a car's headlights

swept across the parking area and she blinked in the harsh glare.

The lights cut off, the engine fell silent and she heard the steady rhythm of a man's footsteps. Maybe he could let her in.

'Eve?'

Hugh.

She turned towards him, her heart kicking against her ribs. 'Did you forget something?'

His smile was crooked. 'It'll keep. What are you doing out here still?'

She sighed in frustration. 'I've been really stupid. I've left my keys in the flat. I've got a spare in my car, but guess what?'

He grinned. 'The spare for your car is in the flat?'

'Bingo. And I'm supposed to be clever enough to save lives?'

His grin got wider, and he propped himself against the glass wall of the foyer and shook his head. 'That's a different part of the brain.'

'Well, there's a mercy. For a moment there I was worried for my patients.'

'No need. They're safe.' He pushed himself away from the wall, stuffing his hands into his trouser pockets and cocking his head on one side. 'So—what now?'

She shrugged. 'You tell me. I can't get in, I can't go anywhere in the car—I guess I'll have to find a hotel for the night and sort it out in the morning.'

'Or you could stay with me.'

Her heart thumped in her chest and she looked at him, her eyes flicking away again, then back. 'Oh. Well—are you sure? That seems…'

'Seems?' he prompted gently.

Her shoulders lifted again. 'An imposition?'

He smiled. 'Oh, come on. I can't have my favourite registrar sleeping in a cardboard box on the doorstep.'

'I'll tell Oliver you said that.'

'What? That I don't want you sleeping in a box?'

'That I'm your favourite.'

He chuckled. 'Oliver's a clever man, he knows. He has all sorts of sterling qualities, but he looks dire in a skirt.'

'And that's enough to make me your favourite?' she said, her professional pride suddenly dented. Maybe he was just like the professor after all.

His eyes were teasing and tender and made her feel funny inside. 'Oh, yes,' he said softly. 'That's enough—that and the fact that you make the best dinner companion I've had for years, and you aren't afraid to put me in my place when you feel it's necessary.' He seemed to relent, his mouth kicking up in a smile. 'Oh, and it doesn't hurt that you're showing all the signs of turning into a damn fine surgeon either.'

She felt her skin warm at his praise, and tried for a teasing note. 'Well. Just keep telling me that until I believe it, and maybe I'll stop looking over my shoulder for Julia and her axe.'

'Axe?' he said, chuckling.

'She's got it in for me. Every time I catch sight of her, her mouth tightens up.'

'Ah.' He looked down, his mouth pursed, then tipped his head on one side in a curiously revealing gesture. 'That may be nothing to do with you and everything to do with me.'

'You— Oh!' She felt a ridiculous and crushing sense of disappointment, but he was laughing softly.

'Oh, no. There's nothing like that. She scares me rigid, but unfortunately it's not mutual. Let's just say she wouldn't have been averse to us getting a little closer.' He glanced around. 'Why are we having this conversation here on your chilly doorstep when we could be curled up on my sofa with a nice cup of tea?'

She hesitated another moment, but it really only was a moment, and she knew she was going to fold like a wet tissue. She really didn't have a lot of options anyway, and, after all, they'd be well chaperoned by his kids.

Safety in numbers, she told herself, and there was little more offputting than nosy teenagers. Maybe with them around she'd be able to resist the urge to lob herself into his arms and kiss him!

He hadn't known if the kids were going to be in. Unlikely, on a Friday night, but Lucy's light was on and Tom's car was in the driveway. For once he was grateful the kids were both around. They could chaperon him, make sure he didn't rush into anything hasty with Eve, he thought as he slipped the key into the lock and opened his front door.

Seconds later he thought better of that random fit of gratitude, as Tom strolled barefoot through the hall, a bowl of cereal in one hand dripping a steady trail of milk across the carpet while his attention was focussed on the book in the other hand.

He looked up just as Hugh reached out and righted the bowl.

'Whoops,' he said with a grin, then caught sight of Eve and the grin widened.

'Hi, there. Had a good meal?'

'Lovely, thank you.'

'Great. Dad, Lucy wants to see you. She's having trouble with her homework.'

'She should be asleep,' he muttered, and turned to Eve, smiling apologetically. 'Give me a minute—make yourself at home in the sitting room.'

'Actually, I could murder a cup of tea. Should I put the kettle on?'

'You're a star,' he said, resisting the urge to drag her into his arms and kiss her senseless. 'Right, Lucy, you've got two minutes,' he muttered under his breath.

He ran up the stairs, losing his tie on the way, and rapped on her door.

'Come!'

'I'm not a dog,' he pointed out, shoving the door open against the heap of clothes. 'I see you're hanging your clothes on the floor again.'

'Yeah, yeah,' she said, and gave him a sleepy grin. 'Any good at biology?'

'Well, now, let me think,' he said drily, and rolled his eyes. 'What do you need to know?'

'I don't understand this bit—it's genetics.'

She thrust an open book in his direction and he stared at it for a second, then gave up.

'I'll sort it out with you tomorrow. It's easy, but it'll take time, and Eve's here. She's locked herself out of her apartment, so I'm glad you're still up. You can go and sort out the spare bedroom. You haven't cleared it up since Amy was here last. There are clean sheets in the airing cupboard and you know where the vacuum is. The bathroom could probably do with a look as well. Don't forget to find her a clean towel, preferably not one of the ones with holes in.'

He left her grumbling in protest, and ran back down to the kitchen, to find Eve making tea and Tom propped up at the island, munching his cereal and watching her.

'You could have made the tea,' he said, but Tom just grinned.

'Nah. She's happy. Who am I to interfere with that?'

He grunted, went over to Eve and took the box of teabags out of her hand.

'Let me,' he said, and she relinquished her hold on them and turned, arms folded over that delectable chest as she propped herself against the worktop and watched him.

Highly distracting. He nearly poured boiling water over his hand, trying not to look at the soft swell of her breasts out of the corner of his eye, and then he mashed the teabags so hard with the spoon that one of them burst.

'You can have that one,' she teased. Taking the other mug from him, she threw most of the contents down the sink, topped the mug up with hot water and smiled indulgently at him. 'Why do men do that?'

'What?'

'Make tea so strong? When I said I could murder a cup of tea, I didn't mean you to take me so literally!'

He grinned. 'My grandmother used to say something about being strong enough to trot a mouse across the top.'

Eve snorted. 'You could trot an elephant across that, Hugh,' she pointed out, and Tom chuckled.

'So where's Kelly?' he asked, as it had suddenly occurred to him that his son was at home alone for a change.

'She's gone home for an early night—felt a bit rough. I think that pill might be working.'

'Good,' he replied, glad that one thing was going right in his life. He really, *really* wasn't ready to be a grandfather at thirty-five! He took the plastic milk carton out of the fridge, peered at it with a sigh and poured a dribble into each mug.

'Did you have enough milk on your cereal?' he asked, his voice tinged with sarcasm, but it was lost on Tom, who simply grunted.

'Uh. Yeah, it was fine.'

Hugh waggled the bottle at him. 'Sure about that?'

Tom eyed the empty bottle, pulled a rueful face and slid to his feet. 'Sorry. There's more in the freezer.'

'Which won't help me now. Finished?'

'Yup.'

'Then put your bowl in the dishwasher and go and give Lucy a hand sorting out the spare room, please, so we can have a few moments at least of relative peace and quiet at the end of a killer week.'

Tom opened his mouth to argue, looked from one to the other and shut it with a grin. 'All *right*,' he said, and, picking up his book, he sauntered off grinning broadly, his bowl still defiantly on the island.

Hugh rolled his eyes, ignored it and ushered Eve through to the sitting room, somehow resisting the urge to put his hand on her delectably lush, sleek bottom.

'Have a seat,' he said, watching as she kicked off those crazy shoes and curled up at the end of one of the sofas. Her skirt slid up, revealing a tantalising glimpse of smooth, pale thigh before she rescued it and tugged it into place. Desire slammed through him.

Music, he thought desperately. He put on a CD—anything to break the silence—and realised after the introductory bar that it was a hopelessly romantic album of Sam Gregory's that he'd been listening to the night before in a lonely and melancholy mood—a mood that had far too much to do with the beautiful and tempting woman sitting opposite him.

At first he was going to stop it, cut it off before she realised what it was, blame it on Lucy, who wouldn't be seen dead listening to something like that. But then he thought, What the hell? We've had a romantic dinner. Why not? And it would surely be easier to sit here and listen to Sam's CD than to try and make conversation in a vacuum when all he could think about was Eve's legs.

But it wasn't easier. She met his eyes, looked away and coloured softly. God, what was she thinking? He wanted to ask her, but he didn't dare, because if it was anything along the lines of what he was thinking, there was no way he wanted to hear it.

Not tonight, when his kids were both around and would be keeping a very close eye on what he was up to.

It was hellish, and when after an interminable time she set down her mug on the coffee-table, he stabbed the remote control and plunged them into a deafening silence.

The kids must have gone to bed, he realised. Or were keeping quietly out of the way. That was a first. And it left them dangerously alone with their undercurrents.

'You must be tired, it's been a long week,' he said eventually, but she didn't smile. She just looked at him, her eyes a little confused and wary, and with a cross between a growl and a sigh, he catapulted to his feet.

'Come on, time you were in bed,' he said, and she

unfolded her endless legs from under that glorious bottom and stood up. At the door to the hall she paused and turned to him, her thoughtful eyes searching his. 'Why did you come back?' she asked softly.

'Back?'

'To my apartment this evening.'

He hesitated. 'I forgot something.'

'What?'

Surrendering to the inevitable, he gave a weary sigh, tired of fighting, and took the small stride that put her in reach. 'This,' he murmured. Lifting his hands, he cupped her face, oh, so gently, and lowered his mouth to hers.

She made a tiny noise, the merest whimper of need, but it unravelled him, and he reeled her in against his chest, threaded his fingers through the glorious waves of her hair and plundered that sweet, soft, open mouth as if his life depended on it.

Oh, dear God, she still tasted of chocolate.

His tongue raided every corner of her mouth, every velvety recess, feeling the sharp, clean edge of her teeth, the warm softness of her lips, the smooth glide of her tongue against his. She eased away, her lips sipping his, tasting him, savouring him for a moment before parting again with a groan and giving him access.

He was going to die. He was. Tonight. Now.

But then she eased away again, her eyes soft and gentle and full of regret.

'Hugh, no. The kids…'

Oh, damn.

He released her abruptly and stepped away quickly, while he still could. 'You're right,' he said gruffly. 'I'm sorry.'

Her fingers came up and pressed against his lips. 'Don't be,' she murmured.

He took her hand in his, pressing her fingers to his lips and closing his eyes, struggling for control. 'I'll show you to your room,' he said at last, and took her upstairs. Lucy and Tom, miraculously, had done a good job of her room, to his relief. There was even a clean towel over the end of the bed, one of the better ones. 'I'll get you a T-shirt,' he said, opening the airing cupboard and pulling out the first one of his he came to. 'Do you need anything else for the night?'

Like me?

Her smile was wry with understanding. 'No, I'll be fine. Thank you.'

He nodded, hesitated a second then brushed her lips with his. 'Goodnight, Eve,' he said, his voice a soft, throaty growl raw with desire.

'Goodnight,' she whispered, and closed the door with the softest click, with him feeling as if he was quite definitely on the wrong side of it.

Rats.

Sleep would have been impossible, so he went downstairs, cleared up the mess the kids had left in the kitchen, loaded the dishwasher and cleaned his shoes, leaving them on the side for the polish to dry. He heard Eve moving around in the room above, heard her in the bathroom, then when all was quiet and he thought he was under control he went back upstairs, his bare feet silent on the stair carpet. Without allowing himself the indulgence of hesitating for a nanosecond outside her bedroom door, he went into his own room, shut the door firmly and went to bed.

* * *

He'd kissed her.

Eve lay there in the quiet house as dawn stole across the sky, listening to the birdsong outside her window, and touched her fingers to her lips.

He'd been coming back to kiss her goodnight.

She closed her eyes and rolled to her side, tugging the pillow tight into her arms. Dear God. If she'd had her keys, if she'd been in her apartment when he'd got back…

They'd be lovers by now. No question about it.

And they were going to be. She knew that, just as she knew the sun would rise in a little while and he would be getting up, showering—

No! Don't think about it. Don't think about hot water streaming over his naked body, coursing through the light scatter of hair on his chest, cascading down that smooth, rigid abdomen, over the rippling muscles and taut flesh, down—

'Eve?'

The tap on the door made her lift her head.

'Yes?'

'I've made you tea.'

'I'll come down.'

'No need, it's here.'

He opened her door a crack. 'Can I come in?'

She was sleeping in the T-shirt that he'd lent her, and so long as she kept her legs in the bed it would be fine. The top she'd worn last night had been more revealing. 'Of course,' she said, wondering why her heart was crashing against her ribs and it suddenly seemed so incredibly intimate.

Not that the room was small. Far from it. It was a lovely, spacious room, but once Hugh was in it, wearing a T-shirt and snug jersey boxers under an open dressing-gown, the walls seemed to shrink. He pushed the door shut with his hip and came over to the bed, two cups in hand, and set one down on the bedside table before hitching a hip on the edge of her bed.

'Sleep all right?'

She decided not to tell him about the hours spent thinking about him. Instead she nodded and smiled. 'Fine, thank you. Much better than I would have in a cardboard box.'

His answering smile was warm and teasing, and all she could think about was kissing him, the feel of his lips, the touch of his tongue…

'God, Eve, don't look at me like that,' he groaned, and she looked up from his full, chiselled lips to meet eyes that blazed with such a fierce need that she almost whimpered in response.

She pushed herself up on her arms, stuffed the pillow into the small of her back and sat up against the headboard, cradling the mug of tea like a lifeline. But they couldn't just sit there drinking tea and pretending the kiss hadn't happened, so with her typical straightforward assault on the obvious, she said, 'This is going to be really complicated, isn't it?'

He sighed and scrubbed long fingers through his sleep-rumpled hair. 'Yes. No.'

'No?' she said, staring at him in confusion. 'How can it not?'

His laugh was ragged and full of frustration. 'I don't know. You're right, it'll be complicated, but so be it. We'll deal with it.'

'So what are we going to do, Hugh?' she asked softly. 'Are we going to pretend that nothing's happening, or—?'

She broke off and he waited, his eyes locked with hers,

and she could see his jaw tensing, his Adam's apple working as he swallowed.

'Or what, Eve?'

She bit the bullet. 'Or are we going to go to bed and get it over with?'

His tea lurched, slopping over onto his fingers, scalding him. He shook them, sucked his index finger ruefully, wiped them on his T-shirt. 'Hell, Eve…'

She shook her head, laughing softly at him. 'Are you OK?'

'No, I'm not OK,' he growled quietly. 'I'm aching with frustration. I want to be alone with you, to make love to you, and my daughter's in the next room and my son's right opposite. How the hell am I supposed to be OK?'

Her heart thumped, but she knew what she was going to do. Her mind might disagree, but it was still asleep, and her heart and her body knew exactly what they wanted. 'I'll get my keys back this morning,' she pointed out. She didn't say any more, but she didn't have to. There was nothing more that needed saying.

His eyes widened, then dropped, fastening on her chest with a hunger that she could almost taste. 'That's my favourite T-shirt,' he said, his voice strangled. 'I'll never be able to look at it again without thinking of you in it.'

She opened her mouth to apologise, then thought better of it. He didn't look exactly sorry after all, and she felt suddenly filled with feminine satisfaction. There was something amazing about being able to put that look on his face, and although she couldn't quite believe it was happening, she wasn't going to knock it. It had been a very long time since anyone she found attractive had been attracted to her. Mutuality seemed almost a foreign concept.

So, no, she wasn't going to knock it, or walk away from it.

Neither was she going to think about it too much, because if she did, if she allowed herself to think too much about the complications, she'd run a mile, and for once in her life she didn't want to do the sensible thing.

At all.

So she smiled, and shifted slightly so that the T-shirt pulled tighter across her breasts. His eyes flared and then shut, a ragged chuckle dragged from his chest.

'You are going to pay for that,' he growled, but before she could reply, he swore softly and stood up, his dressing-gown catching on the bed and pulling open. 'Phone,' he muttered, and walked out, leaving her smiling.

If she'd had any doubt about her effect on him, she'd just had ample proof. Those soft jersey boxers hid absolutely nothing…

Seconds later he was back. 'That was Sam. Molly's in labour, he's taken her to the hospital. I promised I'd get there straight away.'

'Can I come?'

'Sure, if you're quick.'

Without thinking, she threw back the covers, and Hugh's eyes widened and then slammed shut.

'Get dressed,' he muttered hoarsely. 'I'll see you downstairs in five.'

CHAPTER SEVEN

SAM was pacing the floor like a wild man when they arrived, and he pounced on them.

'Find out what's happening,' he demanded. 'She's got a transverse lie and I want to know what they're planning. They threw me out.'

'They?'

'Oliver and Sue. Said I was in the way. Said if I couldn't shut up I had to leave.' His ferocious growl was rendered completely harmless by the concern in his eyes, and Hugh just slung an arm around his shoulders, told him not to worry and went through the door into the delivery suite, taking Eve with him.

Molly was on the bed, Oliver and Sue each side of her, and a monitor was keeping track of what looked to Eve like a nice steady heartbeat.

Hugh kissed Molly on the cheek and scanned the monitor. 'Hi, trouble. How're you doing?'

'I'm livid,' she said fiercely. 'I can't believe it, Hugh, the baby's turned! It's an oblique transverse lie and I'm dilating really slowly as a result, and it hurts like hell, even though I'm getting nowhere fast. If my waters break, I'm going to be right out of options. Damn, I really, really didn't want this, and I'm going to end up with a section, I just know it. I haven't even packed a case yet. I'm not ready for it!'

Her eyes filled with furious tears, and without thinking Eve went over to her and hugged her friend. 'Molly, it'll be OK.'

'I want a normal delivery,' she wailed. 'I've only had one off-the-peg pregnancy. I've had IVF, I've given two babies away—I don't need to add a section to the list!'

'Look on the bright side,' Sue said comfortingly. 'Think of your pelvic floor.'

Molly snorted at her colleague. 'I don't have a pelvic floor any more,' she said bluntly. 'Bonnie took care of that. Hugh, tell me you can turn it.'

Hugh was checking her over while she ranted, feeling her abdomen, listening to her baby's heartbeat, checking the lie with his hands and the portable ultrasound.

Oliver was filling him in. 'She woke at five with contractions every three minutes, and came straight in. I've done an ultrasound, which revealed nothing abnormal, and we've monitored the baby and it's doing fine. But I didn't want to do anything else until you go here. Do you still need me,' he added, 'because I've got a woman in Gynae who needs my attention, if you're happy to take over.'

'I'll take over. You go. Thanks, Oliver.' He sighed, hitched a hip up on the edge of the bed and took Molly's hand. 'Well, you're right, of course. It's a slightly oblique transverse lie. Luckily, it's the head end that's down a bit, but the baby's quite happy and your abdomen's nice and flexible between contractions. I can try and turn it for you, if you like, and that'll only work if you've got enough fluid, but I want you prepped for Theatre, I want an epidural in first and I don't want any arguments if I have to do a section in a hurry.'

Molly stared at him. 'You think you can do it?'

He shook his head. 'I think I can try. That's all. And Sam will want to interfere and try and turn it himself, because he can't delegate for nuts, you know that, and then he'll be yelling for a section if I don't do it first go. This has to be your call.'

She nodded. 'Go for it, Hugh. I really, really don't want a section. And you'd better let Sam back in before he blows a fuse. I'll keep him under control.'

He chuckled and stood up, squeezing Molly's shoulder comfortingly. 'Good girl. We'll get you all set up as quickly as possible. I take it you want an epidural and not a GA if it comes to that?'

She nodded. 'I don't want either, really. Can't we keep an eye on the baby and do an epidural if we have to?'

'We could run out of time.'

'Try turning it once first, Hugh—please? Just in case.'

He sighed, shook his head and winced. 'Sam's going to give me some strain about this,' he muttered, and headed for the door, leaving Molly alone with Sue and Eve.

She flopped back against the pillows, closing her eyes. A tear dribbled out of the corner of one of them, and Eve tutted and sat on the bed, putting her arms round Molly and rocking her gently. She'd grown really fond of the cheerful, unflappable midwife in the past ten days, and she couldn't bear to see her so upset.

'It'll be fine, Molly,' she said, not at all sure that it

would, because she'd never seen Hugh do this and she wasn't convinced it would work. From the sound of it, neither was Sam. He came in with Hugh moments later, still arguing, and she moved out of his way as he gathered Molly up against his chest and hugged her hard.

'God, why did this have to happen to you? You should have stopped work earlier. You're a crazy woman,' he said, his voice choked.

'I know—but I'll be fine. I've seen Hugh do this loads of times. I know it can work. Dammit, you've done it, too, just as often.'

'Yeah, but I won't get the chance to do it, will I? And what if he fails?'

'Hugh won't fail.'

Sam snorted, and Hugh rolled his eyes.

'Such touching faith. Never deliver a colleague's baby,' he said drily to Eve. 'They know far too much for their own good. That's why it's always the consultants that get suckered into it—because that's where the buck stops, and everyone else legs it for the hills. Nightmare stuff.'

'I'm going nowhere, I want to see you do this,' Eve said firmly, and Hugh grinned.

'You just want to see me louse it up,' he teased. 'Right, where's Peter? Let's get this epidural set up ready to go if necessary, and have a shot at turning young master Gregory round.'

'He might be a girl.'

He grinned at Molly. 'Very likely, as she's changed her mind about the presentation. Right, I'm going to put on scrubs. Eve, are you coming to change?'

And then everyone looked at her, taking in the pretty

skirt, the fitting, slinky top, the high heels, and she felt colour bloom in her cheeks.

'Good idea,' she said hastily, and headed for the door.

Damn. He really, really wasn't looking forward to doing this. Molly's faith in him was just a burden, and while he was confident that he had a chance of turning the baby, he couldn't guarantee it.

And Molly wanted guarantees. Molly, of all people, who had to know there could be no guarantees.

Well, he could only do his best, and he'd just have to hope it was good enough. It was a routine enough procedure, to try an external version in early labour in a multiparous woman, but Sam was going to be standing over him, interfering with every breath.

Lord, he hated having to deliver colleagues. It was every doctor's nightmare, and to have a patient who was not only a colleague but also the wife of another colleague, and with this complication chucked in just to liven things up—

'Hugh? It'll be OK.'

He looked at Eve, standing there in her scrubs, looking every bit as desirable as she had in the flirty skirt and slinky top, and knew he was in trouble.

Deep trouble.

No time to think about that now. He summoned a smile. 'I wish I had your faith.'

'You don't have to have faith. You just have to do your job. Leave the faith thing to the rest of us. You can do it. I know you can.'

'How?'

She smiled wryly. 'Because Molly said so. She said she's seen you do it lots of times.'

'It can fail.'

'She knows that, too. She's not being unrealistic. At least she knows what's going to happen.'

He hoped so. Knowing something and having it happen to you were two very different things, as he well knew. 'I'll need your help. I want you to push one end of the baby while I push the other, so we spin it about the centre. Make sense?'

She nodded. 'Just tell me where to push and how hard.'

'And don't let Sam get in the way.'

She laughed at that. 'You think he will?'

'I know he will. I know I would.'

'We'll keep him out of the way. Right, shall we get this show on the road?'

He closed his eyes, centred himself for a moment then nodded. 'OK. Let's go for it.'

They found Peter, the anaesthetist, on standby but on Molly's instructions holding back from giving the epidural. Sam was trying to overrule her and getting nowhere.

'Now, now, children, don't fight,' Hugh said calmly. 'I'll give it one try, then you have the epidural, as agreed. Are you ready, Molly?'

She nodded, but he could tell she wasn't looking forward to it. It could be painful, certainly very uncomfortable, but it would be less painful than recovering from a section, and she'd had time to prepare herself.

Sam, however, was a different matter, and he was pacing restlessly and twitching.

'Sam, go and stand over there by Molly's head and talk to her and be supportive,' Hugh said firmly. 'You're just another father now, you're not a doctor, and if you can't remember that I'm going to duct-tape you to the wall outside and leave you there till it's all over. OK?'

Sam opened his mouth, shut it again and nodded, his mouth twisting into a crooked grin. 'Sorry. I'm used to running the show. I make a lousy voyeur.'

'I forgive you.' Molly chuckled, and he gave her a strained smile and hugged her.

'I'm sorry this has happened, sweetheart.'

'Don't be, it'll be fine. OK, Hugh, I'm ready when you are.'

He was never going to be ready—not with Sam threatening to break out of his box at any moment and Molly pinning everything on him, and Eve— No. Don't think about Eve. Eve's for later, when this was over.

He smiled encouragingly at Molly. 'OK. Let's do it.'

It was amazing.

One moment the baby was stuck sideways, resisting all their efforts, and then Hugh gave one last shove, grunting with effort, and Eve felt the little bottom under her hands shift across and slip neatly under Molly's ribs.

'Got it,' he said, grinning victoriously, and Sam tipped back his head, opened his mouth and let his breath out on a long, ragged sigh.

'That was bloody lucky,' he growled, but Hugh was grinning still and Molly's silent tears of pain and worry were turning to tears of laughter and relief. She was gently stroking her abdomen, wiping off the ultrasound gel they'd used to prevent her skin from getting pulled during the very physical manoeuvre and murmuring softly to her baby.

And Eve—well, Eve was just hugely relieved for Molly that it was over and that the baby had turned without the need for an epidural or any surgical intervention.

But then suddenly things hotted up without warning. Molly's eyes widened, she said, 'Oh, OK, guys, my waters have gone.' There was a sudden rushing of amniotic fluid pouring off the bed and hitting the floor in an impressive stream.

'Wow. Lots of fluid. No wonder it could turn so easily,' Sam said, eyeing it worriedly.

'Is it clear?' Molly was asking, but Sue had other things on her mind, and as she shifted position Eve could see what it was, and her heart lurched.

'It's clear, but, Hugh, the cord's prolapsed.'

Sam leapt forward, but Hugh elbowed him out of the way and took one quick look, swearing softly.

'Right, Molly. You're fully dilated, and you've got two minutes to get this baby out. Do you think you can do it, or do you want to go for a section?'

'Section,' Sam said instantly, but Molly was shaking her head and struggling up off the pillows.

'I can do it,' she said, determination clear in her eyes. 'Sam? Help me up. I need to kneel—now!'

And in the time it took Sam to lift her and turn her so she was draped over the pillows and hanging onto the head of the bed, the baby's head had crowned and Sue was telling her to pant, Hugh was checking that the cord wasn't round the baby's neck. Without waiting for any further instructions, the baby slid into Hugh's hands, yelling his lusty little head off and clearly none the worse for his speedy arrival.

'It's a boy and he's fine,' Hugh said.

Sam turned away, his shoulders heaving, and Eve found herself wrapped in a very hard and very male hug.

'Sorry,' he said, sniffing hard, and she laughed and handed him a tissue and turned him back towards his wife and baby, who was now settled noisily at her breast, the pulsing cord trailing across Molly's soft abdomen. 'Hello, little one,' he said unevenly, and, leaning over, he wrapped Molly in a firm and very loving one-armed hug, the other hand hovering over his son in a gesture so tender it brought a huge lump to Eve's throat.

'Oh, damn,' she whispered, and with a muttered, 'Come here,' she found herself against Hugh's hard, reassuringly solid chest.

'Well done, you,' she mumbled, and he laughed softly.

'A lucky break,' he replied, hugging her close again before releasing her. He turned back to Molly, checking the placenta after Sue had scooped it into a bowl, and nodding with satisfaction.

'That's fine—a bit on the small side, but, then, we expected that as the baby's a bit small for dates.'

'Is he?' Molly said, peering at him. 'They all look smaller than they feel, believe me!'

'Just be grateful he was small. A big baby might have made things much more complicated.'

'A big baby might not have been able to turn so easily,' Molly pointed out with some truth.

The door swung open, and Josh Lancaster walked in, taking in the scene at a glance and rolling his eyes.

'You might have waited for me, Molly,' he said with a grin.

She looked up from the baby with a welcoming smile

for the paediatric consultant. 'You were too slow. You shouldn't have had that extra coffee.'

'Ha-ha. Very funny. I've left skid marks on the road all the way from home.' He bent over and kissed her on the cheek, shook Sam by the hand and ran a gentle finger over the baby's cheek. 'So who's this, then? Anyone going to introduce me?'

'Noah, I reckon, judging by the amount of amniotic fluid.'

Josh cocked an eyebrow at Sam. 'Noah?'

'No,' Molly said with a laugh, slapping Sam on the hand. 'He's Max.'

'Well, little Max, I hate to do this to you, mate, but I need to have a look at you and make sure you're going to be able to count to ten without getting in a muddle. Come to Uncle Josh. Anything I should know?'

'Apart from a prolapsed cord and a very precipitate delivery, buckets of amniotic fluid and an external version? Not really.'

Josh rolled his eyes again, scooped Max up, laid him in the waiting crib and looked down at him sceptically. 'I thought the other day you said you were thirty-five weeks, Molly? Can you lot count?'

Molly chuckled. 'Apparently not. We've gone by the ultrasound dates but they were a bit few and far between,' she confessed. 'Hugh revised it up to thirty-eight yesterday.'

'Good,' Josh said. 'Because I was beginning to think you were all totally incompetent. I reckon he's pretty much full term, even though he's a little on the small side. He's certainly mature enough to cope without problems. What did the scans indicate?'

'I missed one or two,' Molly pointed out. 'Milestone scans, really, because I was too busy either at work or with the kids.'

'The ones you had threw up date anomalies, though, all the way along the line, if you read the reports,' Hugh pointed out, 'but you seemed so positive about the timing, and who am I to disbelieve a midwife and an obstetrician when they tell me when their baby's due? By yesterday it was obvious that you two were just plain wrong. Maybe you need a calendar on your bedside table?'

Sam coloured slightly and grinned. 'We might have made a mistake with the dates, I suppose. We're a bit hit and miss in the common-sense department, and the house is always so busy it's a miracle we found the time to conceive him, never mind keep track of it! As to when it was—does it matter? He's fine, Molly's fine, I need a quiet lie-down to get over it and then I'll be fine. I think it's time for a vasectomy, actually. I think Molly's had enough babies, and I'm damn sure I have! Any repeats of today and I'll be a basket case. Funny how it's just so different when it's your own.'

'Tell me about it.' Josh laughed softly, completing his check of little Max with the hated hip check. With a gentle apology to the protesting baby, he lifted him carefully and handed him back to his mother.

'One gorgeous little fellow, all present and correct. I take it he's been feeding all right in the last few minutes?'

'Fine.'

'Good. Too much amniotic fluid can be a sign of oesophageal atresia, but if he's suckling well and not regurgitating, I think we can safely rule that out. Keep an eye on him, though, and call me if you're worried. I don't think you need to be, not for him, but his head hasn't been moulded a great deal, so I guess you were the one to bear the brunt of it.'

'I don't doubt it,' Molly said a little shakily. 'I'm beginning to feel a bit shocky—it was so fast.'

'You'll be fine. Well done. Can I go and get on with my gardening now, please? Lissa's got plans for this afternoon but if I don't get the lawn cut it'll need a goat to deal with it.'

'Go on, go away,' Molly said with a grateful smile. 'And thanks.'

'My pleasure.' He kissed her again, gave Sam a brief, hard hug and a slap on the back and sauntered out, whistling cheerfully.

'Right,' Hugh said gently. 'Let's have a look at you, Molly. You did really well there to get him out so fast, but I've got a horrible feeling Josh is right and you will have torn.'

'I have. I felt it,' she said, starting to tremble all over with the shock of the rapid delivery.

He checked her very carefully, then nodded. 'Yup. Sorry, love. You'll need a few sutures.'

'I can fix it,' Sue said calmly, taking Molly's hands in hers and rubbing them vigorously. 'Why don't you guys take Sam and feed him some breakfast? I'll look after Molly. She needs a brisk rub-down and a cup of tea, and then we'll worry about the rest. She'll be fine with me.'

'Are you sure?' Sam asked, looking at his shaking wife with concern. Molly pulled him over, kissed him and patted his cheek. 'I'm fine, really. I'll be fine in a minute. It happens all the time. Go on. You can go and plan your vasectomy and Sue and I will finish up here.'

'Coffee first,' he said, looking squeamish at the mention of a vasectomy, 'and a few thousand phone calls. Sue, page me if you need me back here. Right, guys, breakfast is on me.'

He slung an arm around Eve's shoulders and hugged her as they left the room. 'Thanks for turning out for us.'

'You're welcome. Actually, I didn't have a lot of choice. I was at Hugh's, because I managed to lock myself out of my flat last night and I didn't have anywhere to go, but I wouldn't have missed it for the world.'

He gave a hollow laugh and looked at Hugh across the top of her head. 'Thanks for everything,' he said ruefully. 'Sorry I was such a nightmare.'

'Only what I was expecting,' Hugh replied, grinning. 'If you think about it, the external version was a pretty routine procedure on a patient like Molly. You wouldn't have thought twice about having a go on one of your patients. The prolapsed cord made it all a little bit too exciting, though. We could have done without that.'

Sam nodded, pressed the lift button and then looked down at their scrubs. 'You two aren't really fit to go down to the canteen. Why don't you change while I make a quick call, and we'll meet there in five minutes?'

'Good idea,' Hugh agreed, and they parted company, Sam to his office, Hugh and Eve to Theatre to retrieve their clothes.

'That was amazing,' Eve said as they walked back. 'How on earth did you know she'd get the baby out in time? Weren't you worried?'

He gave a strained laugh. 'Just a tad, but it was her fifth delivery, the baby was small, she knew the score, and I've come up against Molly's determination in the past. I was pretty sure she could do it or I would have tipped her up the other way and rushed her into Theatre.'

'And made Sam a happy man.'

He laughed again and hugged her. 'Sam didn't want her

to have a section, he just wanted everything to be all right. His trouble is he knows too much. Right, clothes.'

She put her glad rags back on, wishing she'd worn something a little less clingy and revealing than that top, and rather more sensible shoes, because she was going to have to walk back to her apartment to meet her landlord shortly and, despite her protests to Hugh the night before, they weren't really that comfortable to walk in.

On the way down to the canteen, she phoned her landlord and he agreed to meet her with the keys, but the only time he could do it was immediately, which, of course, scuppered their plans for breakfast.

She put her phone back in her bag and looked up at Hugh. 'That's a shame. I have to go now. I'm sorry.'

'Don't be. Do you want to take my car? I don't really want to leave Molly until I've checked her over again, but you can't walk in those shoes, whatever you say.'

'Would you mind? It's a bit far and I do need to be there fast.'

He pulled out his keys and pressed them into her hand. 'Here. I'll see you later.'

'I can phone you when I'm done and come back for you.'

'Or I could come round when I've finished here in—say, half an hour? Three-quarters?'

And suddenly all their earlier tension that had been diffused by Molly's delivery was back in spades.

'Make it an hour,' she said, her breath catching in her throat.

He nodded, bent his head and brushed his lips lightly over hers. 'One hour,' he promised, and straightened up, his eyes burning. 'I'll be there.'

* * *

'Wow. That looked pretty intense.'

Hugh met Sam's eyes and looked quickly away. 'Uh—yeah.'

'Good.'

'Good?'

'She's just what you need—a sensible, delightful woman with her life all mapped out, who isn't going to make waves at home or try and take over your life and upset your kids. A nice, liberating, short-term relationship with no strings. That's what you want, isn't?'

Hugh frowned. That *was* what he was after—wasn't it? He always had been in the past, ever since he'd lost Jo. No strings, nothing to complicate his already complicated life. And everything Sam was saying made sense, but it sounded so empty—so hollow.

Was that all Eve was offering?

He thought of the way she'd returned his kiss last night, the way she'd been looking at him all morning, and he didn't think so. He wasn't going to argue with Sam, though, not now. Not this morning. In fact, he didn't really want to talk about it at all.

He slung an arm around Sam's shoulders. 'Never mind me, let's go and get your breakfast, then I need to check on Molly and you need to get home and tell the troops.'

And then he could go and see Eve.

It was amazing what you could do in an hour.

She met her landlord at the front door, apologised profusely, retrieved her keys from the hall table, ran to the corner shop and bought milk and a packet of condoms as an afterthought, then came back, stripped the bed and remade it, plumped up the sofa cushions, had the fastest shower on record. She was just pulling on her clothes when the doorbell rang.

'Hello?'

'It's me.'

She pressed the button on the intercom, heard the click and let it go, then went to the door, pausing to zip her jeans and run her fingers through her hair.

Lord, she was so nervous! She hadn't felt like this for years. For ever, maybe.

She flicked her tongue over her suddenly dry lips to moisten them, then opened the door, just as Hugh raised his hand to knock.

He smiled at her, but it was strained, and she opened the door wider and gestured to him to come in.

'Get your keys sorted?' he asked.

She nodded. 'They were on here,' she said, pointing to the table. Then their eyes locked and the strained smile faded from his face, leaving nothing but need, raw and undisguised.

Her heart hitched against her ribs, then settled to a steady thunder. She reached out her hand, placing it on his chest, feeling his heart beat just as fast.

'Oh, Hugh,' she murmured, and then she was in his arms, and his mouth was locked on hers, and she thought she was going to die if he didn't make love to her right now.

She didn't need to worry. There was no way Hugh was letting her out of his arms any time soon. Well, only so he could tunnel his fingers through her hair and anchor her head and slant his mouth more firmly over hers.

Her fingers threaded through the soft, damp strands of hair at the nape of his neck, her other hand sliding down his spine and coming to rest tucked in the waistband of his trousers, urging him against her. He'd showered, she thought inconsequentially, but then she stopped thinking, because with a ragged groan he backed her against the hall wall, one hard, urgent thigh wedging between hers as he ground his hips against her.

Heat flooded her, taking away her strength so she sagged against him with a cry. Without taking his mouth from hers, he hauled her up into his arms, pushed open the bedroom door with his foot and dropped her on the bed, coming down beside her and finding her mouth again with his.

His breathing was ragged, his heart pounding against her chest, and one hand found its way under her soft sweater and curled possessively round her breast. She bucked against him, and he tore his mouth from hers, dragging the jumper over her head and fastening his mouth over one aching, pleading nipple and suckling hard.

She cried out, reaching for him, her hands clawing at his clothes, and then they were naked, hands, lips, tongues everywhere, searching, seeking, until finally he raised his head and stared down at her with wild eyes.

'Condom?' he said economically, and she reached over to the bedside table, her fingers shaking. He took them from her, and moments later he was moving over her, his big, gentle hands cradling her head, his eyes locked on hers as slowly, endlessly, he entered her with one long powerful thrust.

'Hugh!' she cried, and he stroked again, and again, and again, harder, faster, until she was mindless with need, striving, reaching…

'Come with me, Eve,' he said, his voice hoarse with

control, and slowly, like some primeval force, she felt the ripples start, felt her body clench around him, felt the shudder run through him, the sweat break out on his skin as he stiffened and arched against her, her name a harsh plea on his lips.

'Hugh.' She wept, and then she shattered, her body convulsing around his, cradling it, holding him close to her heart as he poured himself into her with a savage cry of triumph.

Then he lifted his head and stared down into her eyes, and she saw that his eyes were glazed with tears.

He lowered his head, brushed the sweetest, gentlest kiss on her lips and rolled to his side, taking her with him, wrapping her hard against his chest while their hearts slowed and the sweat dried on their skin and the echoes of their release faded quietly away, leaving them at peace.

CHAPTER EIGHT

'EVE?'

She rolled her head towards him, her eyes soft with sleep.

'Mmm?'

'I have to go.'

Her eyes opened wider, and she propped herself up on one elbow. 'Really?' she said, her voice laced with regret.

'Really. The kids will be expecting me. We're meeting in town for lunch. Why don't you come?'

Some unnamed emotion clouded her face and she looked away. 'I don't think so.' She sat up, wrapping her arms around her knees, the quilt falling away to reveal the smooth, warm curve of her breast. He ached to touch it, to lean over and stroke the fine, delicate skin with his tongue, but he didn't have time. If he touched her, let himself reach out…

'Why not? They won't mind if you join us. They'd like to see you again. They both seem to like you.'

She shook her head. 'It's too soon, Hugh. They'll take one look at us and they'll know.'

'Know what?' he asked, wondering how she'd reply, but she just shrugged.

'That we've spent the morning in bed,' she said frankly,

and while he shouldn't have been surprised, and it was, after all, only the truth, nevertheless he felt a little shaft of disappointment.

Stupid. What had he been hoping she'd say? That the kids would know they were in love? Crazy. Ridiculous! They'd only met nine days ago, worked together less than a week. Of course they weren't in love! He was just feeling sentimental because of Sam and Molly and the baby.

He threw back the quilt and stood up, starting to gather his clothes together. 'Maybe you're right,' he said. 'How about coming for lunch tomorrow?'

'Why don't you come here?'

His body reacted with enthusiasm, and with a growl of frustration he rounded up the rest of his clothes, yanked them on and turned to face her again. 'Because I don't want this to be all there is for us—just a hole-in-the-corner affair, sneaking around behind my children's backs.'

'I don't want to sneak, Hugh,' she said, her face troubled. 'I'm just not ready to go public. What will they think?'

He had no idea. He didn't really understand his need to parade her in front of them, unless it was something to do with testosterone and proving to his apparently sexually active son that he wasn't over the hill yet.

And that was something he really ought to think about before he dragged Eve into it.

He scrubbed a hand round the back of his neck and sighed. 'Maybe you're right,' he muttered.

'So when will I see you again?'

He gave a hollow laugh, because he was wondering just how soon he could decently—or indecently!—escape from his family. 'The kids are bound to be out tonight. They always are on Saturday. How about eight?'

'I could cook for you.'

'Then I won't be able to eat with the children, and they'll realise I'm eating out.'

'So don't eat too much, and I'll do dessert.'

He surrendered on a huff of laughter, bent over and kissed her soft, willing mouth very thoroughly. 'Dessert it is. I'll see you at eight.'

It was the start of a wonderful interlude.

At least for Eve it was wonderful. She wasn't so sure how Hugh felt about it. He was the most amazing lover. Tender, passionate, very physical and totally at ease with both her body and his. She'd never had a lover like him before, and if she allowed herself to think about it, she knew she never would again.

But sometimes, after they'd made love, she would catch an expression in his eyes that made her heart ache. It was almost as if he wanted to tell her something and didn't quite know how, as if he hadn't yet worked it out.

She had. He was falling in love with her, and the thought horrified her.

It would never work for them. She couldn't love him. It was impossible. She had her career to think of, and love and her career were mutually exclusive. She had things to do, goals to achieve—promises to fulfil. Promises that at times now were beginning to seem intolerably demanding and crushing in their importance. And anyway, the last thing on earth she wanted was to be involved with the father of two highly vocal and free-thinking teenagers!

Well, no, that wasn't quite true. She didn't mind being involved with their father, but the kids themselves—no way. She remembered the strain of her own upbringing, the endless times she'd covered for her brother, lied for him, run interference so her father didn't kill him while all the time nothing she did was good enough. For years she'd been the mediator, and she didn't want to be involved in all that again, reminded of such an unhappy time in her life.

Her younger brother had been hell as a teenager, and they'd all been miserable—her father, a brilliant doctor and an absolutely lousy and unintuitive parent, her mother, trapped at home, looking after them all and deeply resentful, her brother, once perfect in her father's eyes but now running wild, irritated by his goody-two-shoes big sister who was all there was between him and the thrashing he probably deserved.

He hadn't been nearly as out of control as he would have liked them to think, but bad enough that his exam results had reflected his lack of commitment. Bad enough that his father's continual disappointment had had serious foundation, at least until it had been too late and he'd been dying.

And it hadn't mattered what she'd done, how hard she'd worked, how much she'd tried to be the son he'd wanted in place of the son he'd got. There had been no way he'd believed she could do what she'd promised she'd do. So she'd set out instead to prove it to herself, and she was going to do it, but it had been a hard road, and it had started when she'd been Lucy's age.

No, she didn't want anything to do with teenagers, she'd had a basinful, and she had the sense to realise that Hugh and his kids were a package.

So she didn't allow herself to think about it, and whenever she caught that look in his eyes she distracted him with a kiss, a touch, and he would make love to her again, and the look would go from his eyes for a while, driven out by the raw, fundamental need that never seemed to abate.

And because she didn't allow either of them to dwell on anything too deep, that first week was unadulterated bliss. The days were busy, but because they were working together they saw each other frequently, and the evenings, when they weren't on call, were spent at her apartment, a few snatched hours at a time.

Hours of utter self-indulgence and hedonistic delight. And since it showed no signs of burning out any time soon, and they were in constant danger of running out of condoms, she suggested she should go on the Pill.

'Good idea,' he said with a grin. 'Go to the sexual health clinic at the hospital tomorrow. They've got a walk-in clinic. Then we won't have to worry about accidents.'

She hadn't been, but since he'd mentioned it, she got up the following morning and headed for the hospital. If she got there nice and early, she wouldn't have to wait so long.

That was the theory. She wasn't the only one with the idea, however, and she'd reckoned without the fact that it was the Easter weekend and there were two bank holidays when the clinic was closed. So it was ridiculously busy, and she'd been there an hour and was wondering if it wouldn't be quicker to register with a GP and do it that way when she realised that it would definitely have been the better option, because Tom Douglas strolled in, his arm around the shoulders of a pretty girl about his age, and did a mild double-take.

'Eve—fancy seeing you here,' he said, his smiling face

alive with undisguised curiosity. 'This is Kelly, by the way. Kel, this is Eve Spicer, Dad's new registrar.'

She swallowed her embarrassment, and managed a smile. 'Hi, Kelly,' she said. 'Nice to meet you.' She was on the point of telling them that she was there waiting for a patient's notes when a nurse blew her escape route out of the water by picking up a set of notes and turning towards the crowded room.

'Eve Spicer?' she said, and Eve had no option but to stand up and follow her, leaving Tom and Kelly no doubt speculating on the reason for her visit.

With any luck they'd think it was just a routine check, and that she was already in a relationship with someone else.

Please, God!

'Guess who we bumped into in the clinic at the hospital this morning?' Tom said casually, propping his feet on the island and leaning back on the tall kitchen stool.

'Who?'

'Eve.'

Hugh sliced neatly through the end of his finger, and swore, sticking it in his mouth and squeezing the edger of the cut together with his teeth. Not because it needed it so much as because it occupied his mouth and took away the opportunity to reply—an opportunity he was not in a hurry to take up!

'Really?' he said finally, peering at his finger and swearing softly again. He ran it under the tap, swiped it with a wad of kitchen roll and stuck a plaster on it.

'I hope you haven't bled on the sandwiches,' Tom said cheerfully, and Hugh could have killed him.

'You could always help,' he pointed out.

'Nah. Had enough gory stuff today. Kel had an implant,' he said, and Hugh swivelled round and studied his son thoughtfully.

'Is she OK?'

'Yeah. It was pretty gross, I had to look away. It might get sore when the local wears off, the doctor said. She's got a pressure bandage on it.'

'Yes, she will have. If her fingers swell, I'll slacken the bandage a little. They always seem to do them too tight.'

'Eugh, yuck!' Lucy said, coming in and looking at his finger and the pile of bloodstained kitchen roll beside him. 'You've cut yourself—it's still bleeding.'

'A doctor already,' Hugh muttered, ripping off the plaster and hunting for Steristrips so he could pull the edges of the wound together. It was right on the end of his left index finger, and it would be a real pain while he was operating in the next few days.

'So who does what too tight?' Lucy asked, plopping herself down next to Tom, and Hugh met his eyes and gave an expressive 'over to you' shrug.

'Pressure bandages. Kel's had a contraceptive implant,' he said, managing to look his sister in the eye and only colouring slightly.

Lucy's eyes widened and her mouth made a perfect O. But with commendable restraint she simply said, 'I hope she's OK. Andy's sister got one and it went septic.'

'Oh, cheers, Luce. Kelly'll be thrilled to hear that. I'll be sure and tell her!'

'Sorry! I was just warning you.'

'Well, don't.'

Hugh held his breath. He wasn't sure if Tom had wanted Lucy to know, but at least what was going on between her brother and Kelly was now out in the open.

His relationship with Eve, however, was a different matter, and he really, really didn't want to get into that, but the conversation seemed to have moved away from such dangerous territory. He was about to heave a sigh of relief when Tom continued blandly, 'Seems a lot of people go there. Amazing who you can bump into.'

'Oh, yeah? Who?' Lucy asked guilelessly, and Hugh held his breath. If he so much as glanced warningly at Tom, he'd give the game away, and if he didn't and Tom said something…

Either way, he was in the mire up to his neck and he wasn't going to come up smelling of roses!

'Oh, just the odd person we've seen about,' Tom said airily. 'Dad, can I borrow some money? I seem to have run out.'

'I don't know what you spend it on,' Lucy grumbled. 'Dad, are those sandwiches for us? I hope you didn't bleed on them.'

'No, I didn't. How much?'

He turned and met his son's mocking eyes full on, and Tom shrugged. 'Whatever you think.'

'I think you have a damn cheek.' Tom arched a brow, and Hugh sighed shortly. 'Tom, you owe me big time as it is.'

'I do?'

'You do. Let me remind you about last Monday.'

Tom opened his mouth, shut it again and shrugged. 'A tenner'll do.'

'Good. And it's a loan.'

Lucy tipped her head on one side and scowled at her

brother indignantly. 'What happened on Monday? Did he get more money off you, Dad? That's so unfair, he gets so much more than me!'

'You don't do badly. I seem to remember a certain ski trip,' he pointed out, and she grinned and subsided.

The phone rang. Lucy picked it up, said, 'Hi, Amy,' and wandered off with the handset, leaving Hugh alone with his son.

'So—what do you suppose Eve was doing there?' Tom asked casually, clearly not ready to let the subject drop.

Hugh gave a short sigh and turned to his son, sick of the subterfuge. Wake up and smell the coffee, Tom had said. Well, that cut both ways.

'What *exactly* do you want to know, Tom?' he asked bluntly, expecting his son to back off. But not a bit of it.

He met his father's eyes with a level look and said just as bluntly, 'Are you sleeping with her?'

'Yes.'

Tom's jaw dropped, and he gave a surprised huff of laughter. 'Wow! Go, Dad! Excellent!'

Hugh didn't think so. He didn't want his son speculating about his private life, and he certainly didn't want Lucy knowing about it. 'Look, I don't think Lucy—'

'She's guessed. She said yesterday she reckoned you were. Too many meetings and getting called in. You forget, Dad, we know your schedule. We aren't stupid, and you've had that look on your face that you get when you're having an affair.'

It got worse. Hugh closed his eyes and swore, and Tom chuckled.

'You're saying that word a lot these days,' he teased,

and Hugh sighed and scrubbed his hand round the back of his neck.

'Tom, for God's sake, cut me a little slack here. We're trying to be discreet, because we don't want everyone to know, and I certainly don't want Eve knowing you know. And, anyway, what do you mean, that look I get when I'm having an affair?'

'Oh, come on, Dad, it's not the first time, is it? We aren't stupid.'

Oh, hell. Did they have the spies out, or was he just really lousy at hiding things? Both, probably.

His mobile phone rang, and he flicked it open, wanting privacy but not able to get it without another confrontation. 'Hi there.'

'Hi. Can you talk?'

'Not really.'

'I just wanted to warn you, I bumped into Tom and Kelly at the clinic.'

'I know.'

There was silence for a second, then she said softly, 'Ah. Problems?'

He gave a strangled laugh. 'Only slightly,' he confessed, then decided that since the cat was well and truly out of the bag, he may as well stop pussy-footing around. 'Eve, what are you doing tonight?'

'I don't know. I was waiting for you to suggest something,' she said cautiously. 'Are you alone now?'

He looked at Tom and sighed. 'No chance. I was going to suggest you come here tonight. I'll cook—it's my turn.'

'Oh, rats, they've worked it out, haven't they?'

'Yup. Seven-thirty?'

'Hugh, is it wise?'

'Probably not, but it's just tough. I'll pick you up.'

He ended the call and met Tom's eyes. 'Do something for me, please,' he said seriously. 'Treat my relationship with Eve with respect, as I have done yours with Kelly. I haven't told anyone, I haven't talked about it, I haven't discussed it with your sister or teased you or blackmailed you. I'd be grateful if you'd extend us the same courtesy, for Eve's sake if not for mine. This isn't a cheap affair, Tom, and I don't want you treating it like one.'

Tom swallowed, nodded and slid off the stool looking shamefaced. 'Sure. Sorry. I didn't mean to do that.' He jerked his head towards the sandwiches. 'So—are we going to eat them, or just watch the edges curl up?'

Eve's stomach was in turmoil.

She was having a meal at Hugh's house tonight, possibly with his children present, and they knew. They'd be looking at her with that knowing look, and speculating, and it made her feel sick.

It would be different if she was being introduced to them as his future wife, but his lover—that just made her feel so uncomfortable.

Not that she wanted be his wife at all, or have to bring up his kids. After watching her mother struggle with Andrew for years, even the thought of being a stepmother to a teenage tearaway was enough to bring her out in hives.

She rang Molly, just for something to fill the time and because she was feeling guilty for neglecting her since the baby's birth, and Molly was delighted to hear from her.

'Are you busy, Eve?' she asked. 'Sam's on call and he's had to go into the hospital, and Debbie, our childminder, has taken the kids out for a walk. And of course Max is grumbly and won't settle, and frankly another human being around the place would be lovely!'

So she went, following Molly's directions, and pulled up a few minutes later outside a pretty red-brick cottage with roses around the door. Not that they were blooming yet, but they would be soon, just adding to the idyllic setting for a blissful family.

It was all too perfect, and it made Eve feel panicky, but the feeling eased when Molly wandered round the corner of the house with the baby in her arms and gave Eve a great big smile and a hug. 'Hi, stranger! How lovely to see you. How are things?'

'Busy,' she said, wondering if she should tell Molly about Hugh, but she didn't need to. Molly looked into her eyes searchingly and nodded.

'You look well. Being with Hugh obviously suits you—and it's about time he found a woman.'

Eve shook her head in protest. 'Molly, it's not like that.'

'Of course not. You're going to tell me you're just good friends, and I'm going to nod sagely and let you carry on believing it,' she said with a grin.

'I wasn't going to tell you any such thing!' Eve denied. 'I had no intention of talking about Hugh at all! I've come to see you and the baby. Here, this is for you,' she said, handing Molly a bunch of flowers, a card and a hastily wrapped teething ring rattle she'd been clutching for the past few minutes. 'I should have come before, but I've been so busy—' She broke off, colouring, because Molly was smiling knowingly and, dammit, she was absolutely right about why Eve hadn't found the time!

'So,' she said, hastily changing the subject, 'how's the baby? Sam said he was OK and there was no sign of any problems with him, but I know Josh was a bit worried because of the amount of fluid.'

'Oh, he's fine. No problems with his oesophagus, or anything else for that matter. He's eating for England, and if he carries on like this he's going to be enormous. I think my placenta might have been a bit on the rough side, to be honest, but I have no idea why. Old scarring, maybe, from a previous pregnancy? Goodness knows, there have been enough of them. But he's fine now, we both are, and frankly I'm just glad it's all over.'

'You gave us a bit of a scare with the prolapsed cord,' Eve told her, and Molly gave a wry laugh.

'Gave me a scare, too,' she replied, 'and I don't think Sam will ever get over it. He's seriously talking about a vasectomy, you know. He really doesn't want to have any more. That scared him to bits. Either that or the baby crying all night has reminded him that we didn't really want another anyway!'

They reached the back door, and Molly pushed it open and led Eve into a lovely big farmhouse kitchen, with a huge table in the centre of the room where she could just imagine them all gathered, laughing and talking and arguing, just one big happy family. Just the thought filled Eve with a mixture of envy and dread.

'I'll put the kettle on,' Molly said, 'and you can tell me all about work. How are things going with Hugh—apart from the obvious?'

'Fine—and it's not obvious.'

'If you say so,' Molly murmured, laying the flowers on the sink and filling the kettle one-handed while she jiggled the grizzling baby. 'So—how is it going?'

Suddenly unable to keep up the pretence any longer, she blurted out, 'Oh, Molly, I've got a problem,' and Molly nodded sagely.

'I thought so. Never mind, we'll have a nice cup of tea and talk about it. Have you had lunch?'

Had she? She wasn't sure. 'I don't think so, not what you could call lunch, but I'm not really hungry, to tell you the truth, and I'm having supper with Hugh and the kids tonight.'

Molly studied her for a moment, head tipped on one side, then sighed. 'You look like a lamb to the slaughter. What's wrong with having supper with his kids? Are they so dreadful?'

'No,' she said miserably. 'It's just going to be really awkward. They know—well, that we're sleeping together,' she said, colouring. 'Well, Tom does, anyway.'

'How?'

She couldn't tell her, of course, not without revealing things about Tom and Kelly that weren't hers to reveal, so she just shook her head. 'Let's just say they found out, and now he wants me to go round there this evening and make polite conversation, and all the time Kelly and Tom will be looking at us and thinking…'

'Thinking what? They're not really kids any more, Eve. They're surrounded by sex. It's everywhere. They won't think anything of it. They'll just be checking you out.'

'As what? A potential stepmother? I don't think so. It isn't even on the cards.'

Molly gave her a thoughtful look and poured boiling

water on the teabags without commenting. But it didn't stop her mind working, Eve realised, and she wished she hadn't said anything.

'It's early days,' Molly said quietly. 'Don't get ahead of yourself. Tom's a nice boy, and Lucy's lovely. She babysits for us when Debbie and Mark are away—they're our live-in safety net, but every now and again they remind us they're entitled to a life, and Lucy steps in. The kids adore her, and she's a darling. Tom's a bit more of a handful, but I think he's so like Hugh he can't get more than half a step ahead of his father, and most of the time they get on like a house on fire.'

Great. A lovely, close-knit unit, with her on the outside—which was, of course, just where she wanted to be. If she had any sense she'd have her running shoes on by now, getting the hell out of it, instead of going round there for supper and sandpapering the wounds.

Molly laid a hand on her arm. 'Eve, just enjoy your time with him. You're moving on in a few months. It's not as if he's asked you to marry him, has he?'

She shook her head, not even allowing the thought to come to rest. 'Good grief, no! And I hope he won't, because there's no way!'

'Eve, what is it you're so frightened of?' Molly asked gently, getting right to the heart of it as usual. 'Is it the kids, or commitment, or the idea of marriage, or what?'

'I'm not frightened,' she lied. 'I just don't want to get involved with anyone at the moment. I've got to get through my FRCS exams and get a consultancy before I start worrying about settling down.'

'Why?'

Eve stared at her. 'Why what?'

'Why do you have to do all that before? Why not during, or after? As well as?'

Eve stared at Molly as if she was talking Russian. 'Well—because I can't! It wouldn't be fair on anyone. And, anyway, this is a ridiculous conversation, because there's no way it's going to happen. We're just lovers, Molly. We're having an affair, that's all.'

'Whatever you say,' Molly replied softly. 'Here—tea. And I have a feeling there are some rather lovely chocolates kicking around somewhere. Let's go and top up our iron. Did you know chocolate is a good source of iron? That's why women crave it so much at the time of their periods. And childbirth is just another massive waste of haemoglobin, so I've got lots of topping up to do!'

And, bless her heart, she didn't say another word, just fed Eve chocolates and tea and let her cuddle little Max, and as Eve stared down into his tiny, perfect features, she felt a huge ache building in her chest.

If only her life wasn't so mapped out. If only Hugh didn't have kids already. If only she hadn't promised her father, made herself this stupid timetable that she was so determined to stick to if it killed her…

'It'll be all right, Eve,' Molly murmured, touching her shoulder gently. 'Don't cry.'

She hadn't even realised she was.

'I love him,' she said tearfully.

'I know.'

'I can't, Molly. I can't do it. It scares me to death, and anyway I promised.'

'Who?'

She gulped, took a steadying breath, bit her lip to hold back another wave of tears. 'My father. He was dying. My brother always disappointed him so much, and I thought if I could do it…'

'Do what?'

'Be a doctor. He wanted my brother to follow in his footsteps, and he'd watched him wasting his life with disappointment in his eyes, and so I told him I'd do it. Work harder, pass my exams, become a doctor. A surgeon. A good one, I told him. The best. And I'm going to do it, Molly, I have to, and I can't let Hugh get in the way.'

Molly reached over and lifted Max from Eve's arms, settled him into his crib and then gathered Eve into her warm and motherly embrace. 'My poor, poor girl,' she said softly, rocking Eve while she cried stupid, scalding tears of grief and frustration and guilt. And Molly, bless her, didn't say another word, just let her cry, and then mopped her up and took her for a walk in the garden, showing her the flowers, the apple tree, sitting with her in the spring sunshine and letting the emotional storm recede.

A car pulled up on the drive, and Molly stood up. 'It's Sam. Are you OK now, or do you want a bit longer?'

She shook her head. 'I'm OK. I'm sorry.'

'Don't be. My guess is you've needed to get that out for a long time. Come and have another cup of tea. Sam'll be dying for one.'

Eve followed her slowly, giving her time to greet her husband with a hug and a kiss. She didn't know if Molly said anything to him, but he glanced up at her and smiled and said nothing about her tear-stained face or the rather wobbly smile that was all she could come up with.

'How's the baby?' he was asking, and Molly laughed.

'Quiet now, at last.'

'Excellent. Ten minutes' peace. God, what a hectic day. I've had one emergency after another, and I feel drained.' He flopped down into a kitchen chair, yawned hugely and stretched his long legs out across the floor, his eyes closed.

'He'll be asleep in a minute and get a crick in his neck,' Molly said fondly, but Eve had seen enough. Sam was tired, Molly needed a rest, and she herself didn't need any more domestic bliss this afternoon. Anyway, she was feeling a little foolish after unravelling all over Molly like that, and she wanted to crawl away and hide for a while.

'I'm off now, Molly,' she said softly. 'Thanks for the tea.'

And sympathy.

The words hung in the air, and Molly gave a gentle smile, nearly reducing Eve to tears again. 'You're welcome. Thank you for the baby's present—I haven't even opened it. How rude of me, I'm sorry.'

'Don't be silly, it's nothing.'

'Come and see me again soon. I feel a bit cut off at the moment.'

'Baby blues?'

Molly smiled. 'A bit. And with the other three running around, I'm not exactly resting!'

'You take care. I'll see you soon.'

She kissed Molly's cheek and left, driving home via the supermarket. If she was going to Hugh's for supper, she ought to take something—a bottle of wine, some flowers, chocolates. No, not chocolates. She'd eaten so many at Molly's that even the thought turned her stomach.

Wine, then. That was safe. And flowers, just because nobody ever took men flowers, and it seemed unfair.

She arrived home at six-thirty, showered and was about to dry her hair when her entryphone buzzed.

'Hello?' she said, glad that whoever it was couldn't see her wrapped only in a towel with her wet hair stuck all round her face.

'Eve, it's me. Can I come up?'

'Hugh—um, sure, of course.'

Damn. She'd wanted to get herself together more, to put on her make-up and get her emotional ducks in a row, but he was there, at the door, and gathering her gently into his arms and hugging her, soggy towel and all. 'I'm sorry, I'm horribly early, but I just wanted to make sure you were all right. I rather dumped all that on you earlier, and I've been feeling guilty. I came round at five, but you weren't here.'

'I was at Molly's,' she said, easing out of his arms and flashing him a quick smile. 'Let me throw on some clothes and dry my hair or it'll just go into a mass of curls.'

'Good. I love curls.' And he reached for her again, drawing her back into his arms, his lips finding hers and sipping, stroking, trailing a line of fire over her jaw, her collar-bone, down to the top of the towel, then his fingers were freeing the towel, letting it slide to her feet. 'You are so beautiful,' he said gruffly, then with a ragged sigh he drew her back into his arms and kissed her again.

'We'll be late, the kids will know what we're doing,' she protested, and he lifted his head.

'Does that worry you?'

'Yes. No. I don't know.'

He grinned a little off-kilter and let her go. 'Me, too. Go on, get dressed and let's get this over with. It'll be fine.'

She didn't believe him for a moment, but she dried her hair, pulled on her clothes and came out of the bedroom to find him standing in her kitchen, looking at the flowers.

'Got an admirer?' he asked, inclining his head towards them, and she thought she saw a flash of jealousy.

She debated teasing him, but then thought better of it. 'They're for you,' she told him, feeling a little foolish now. 'I've got you a bottle of red as well, but it's probably horrible, knowing my skill with wine. That's why I got the flowers.'

'I'm sure it'll be fine,' he said, frowning down at the colourful spring bouquet. He reached out and touched the blooms with gentle fingers, then lifted his head, and she saw that he was really struggling. 'They're lovely. Thank you,' he said, his voice gruff.

'You probably think I'm silly, but nobody ever gives men flowers, and they were so pretty…'

His smile was crooked. 'I don't think you're silly at all,' he said, reeling her into his arms and burying his face in her neck. 'They *are* lovely, and so are you, but if you really, really want to get out of here in the next hour or so, we'd better go now, before I change my mind and drag you off to bed…'

CHAPTER NINE

MOLLY was right, Hugh's kids were really very decent young people.

Kelly was there, too, and Eve wondered if she'd say anything about having bumped into met her at the clinic, but she just said, 'Hi, Eve,' in a friendly way, and that was that. Nothing to trigger Lucy's curiosity.

Although she'd probably told her by now, if Tom hadn't. It would have been only natural for them to talk about their discovery while Hugh had been collecting Eve. But there was no suggestion that they had, not a single curious look, nothing to indicate that anything had changed, and after a few minutes Eve found to her surprise that she was relaxed and enjoying their lively and cheerful company.

The only slightly worrying moment came when they were about to eat. They were in the kitchen, collecting dishes and plates to take through to the dining room, and Hugh frowned at Kelly's fingers. 'That pressure bandage is too tight,' he murmured. 'Come here, let me loosen it for you.'

And with deft, gentle fingers, the fingers Eve had come to know so well, he unwound the fine stretchy bandage on her left upper arm and reapplied it, still firmly enough to hold the implant in place but not so firmly that it cut off Kelly's circulation and made her hand swell. 'Better?' he asked, and Kelly nodded, flexing her fingers with relief.

'Much better. Thank you, Hugh.' She smiled shyly at Eve and said, 'I had an implant today. I had to have one. I've got a brain like a sieve, but I'd much rather be on the Pill.'

Eve's heart hiccuped. What was she supposed to say to that? Tell Kelly that, yes, she'd rather be on the Pill, too, which was why they'd given her a prescription at the clinic and she'd taken her first one this evening at six-thirty? She was struggling for some noncommittal reply when Tom chipped in, to her relief.

'I'd much rather you had the implant, or eighteen years down the line this could be us,' he said with a chuckle, and Hugh rolled his eyes.

'Please, God, no. I'm not old enough to be a grandfather. I'm not even sure I'm old enough to be a father yet!'

'Oh, poor Grandpa,' Lucy teased, patting him on the head, and he ducked and swatted her retreating behind.

'That'll be quite enough of that, madam,' he said. 'Come on, the food's going to get cold.'

And he ushered them through to the dining room, the moment safely past, and Eve relaxed again and allowed herself to enjoy the rich, delicious casserole Hugh had cooked for them. It was such a pleasure to eat something like that. Living alone meant eating things cooked in small portions, with no big hearty family meals like this ever getting with spitting distance of her menu, but she didn't envy him having to get home at the end of a busy day and cook for three or four people, every night of the week.

And the food shopping must be a nightmare, she thought, marvelling that he managed to do it all and hold the family together with such a busy and demanding job. They were a credit to him, she realised, and he was a warm and wonderful father to them both.

She felt overawed by it—by the logistics of it, by the warmth and affection and obvious love that ran like threads of gold through every aspect of their relationship. What would it have been like, she wondered, to have been brought up by a father like Hugh? He never, ever, looked at Lucy as if she was a disappointment.

Tears stung her eyes, and she blinked them away quickly and forced herself to concentrate on the conversation. Not that it was exactly demanding. Tom and Kelly were debating where they were going later, and Lucy was telling Hugh about Amy's latest exploits with a boy she'd never heard of, and all she had to do was listen.

'Hey, let's go clubbing!' Kelly said finally. 'Hugh, why don't you and Eve come with us? That would be wicked, seeing the old folks boogie!'

Hugh groaned and laughed. 'Good grief. I'm not sure I'm up to being the entertainment, are you, Eve?'

She shook her head, smiling ruefully. 'Sorry. It's not top of my list. Too old, I guess.'

'That's crazy, you aren't old! How old are you? I bet you're not even thirty yet,' Kelly said with the refreshing honesty of youth.

'Twenty-seven,' she replied, and watched Tom work it out.

'That's really weird. I'm almost eighteen, and Dad's thirty-five, so you're just about halfway between us. Wow.'

'Is that meant to make me feel older or younger?' Hugh

asked drily. 'Because I have to say it makes me feel a heck of a lot older than all of you.'

'Oh, poor old man,' Eve teased, and his mouth twitched.

You'll pay for that later, his eyes seemed to say, and she had to bite her lips to stop the laughter from bubbling up.

'So, as watching the old folks make fools of themselves is clearly off the agenda, where *are* you going?' he asked, changing the subject back again, and the wrangling continued until they'd agreed a venue that Hugh felt was appropriate for Lucy as well. Finally they set off, after arranging to collect Amy on the way and promising to be back at a reasonable hour.

As the door slammed behind them at last, Hugh sagged against the wall and rolled his eyes laughingly. 'They can be such hard work.'

'They're lovely,' she said, surprised that she meant it. Not that she wanted to look after them, ever, but for the odd meal, they were fine.

'They are lovely,' he agreed, 'but they're relentless. Come on, let me take you home. We've got about two hours of peace and I intend to take advantage of every second of them.'

'What about the clearing up?' she said, staring in dismay at the kitchen, but he shook his head.

'I'll do it later. Come on, time to see just how old this old man is,' he said, pulling her into his arms and kissing her. His eyes sparkled with laughter and promise, and Eve felt her breath catch in her throat.

She eased closer to him, feeling his body's instant response. 'Do we have to waste time moving to mine? Can't we just stay here?'

He shook his head. 'No. Knowing my luck, one of them will have forgotten something and they'll come back and catch us, and I really, really don't think I feel ready for that yet!'

'No,' Eve agreed hastily. That was absolutely the last thing she wanted. Knowing was one thing. Living proof was quite another!

That weekend heralded a change in their relationship.

Although they still spent many wonderful, intimate hours in her apartment, they also spent time at his house, both with and without the company of his children, and to her surprise Eve didn't find it nearly as bad as she'd expected.

But they were busy at work, and Hugh was putting more and more responsibility on her, so their down time was pretty limited. Work, however, was anything but limited.

She'd done sections, repairs, amniocenteses, forceps and ventouse deliveries, and she'd done a difficult hysterectomy for fibroids with only minimal help.

Then one morning when she was down in A and E, the young SHO caught her as she was leaving. 'I've just seen a patient with abdo pain—it looks like a classic appendix but she's had a positive pregnancy test. Can you have a look?'

Her blood ran cold. Appendix, or ectopic? 'OK, what's the story?'

'Pain in the right iliac fossa, sweating, slightly pyrexial, nausea, vomiting.'

'Any blood loss?'

'No—I don't think so. Her blood pressure's fine, but I'd like you to take a look at her. I'm pretty sure it's a straight appendix, but I didn't want to take any chances.'

'No. I agree. Let me see her. What's her name?'

'Jenny Field.'

She went into the cubicle, assessing the patient visually as well as shuffling the information the SHO had given her. The patient was pale, with spots of colour on her cheeks and a faint sheen of sweat on her skin. Eve smiled at the young woman and put her hand comfortingly on her shoulder. 'Hi, Jenny, I'm Eve, I'm a gynae registrar. I just want to have a look at you and ask you a few questions, if I may?'

Jenny nodded, answered as well as she could and cried out when Eve palpated her abdomen. She had rebound tenderness, but the pain was continuous, and with appendicitis she might have expected it to come and go a little. It was looking more and more like an ectopic, and she was determined not to mess this up. 'OK, I think the first thing I want to do is an ultrasound to have a look and see what's going on.'

'I thought it was appendicitis. What do you think it is?' Jenny asked worriedly.

'I'm not sure. It might be something to do with the pregnancy, or it could still be appendicitis. The ultrasound will tell us. When was your last period?'

'About two months ago, maybe a bit more? I'm not very regular.'

'OK. I'll just arrange a few tests, and I'll be back.'

Eve bleeped Hugh. He was in Theatre but he should be finished by now, and she needed his expertise.

'I'm in A and E. Query ectopic,' she told him, and he came down so fast she knew the alarm bells were ringing.

'How's she presenting?'

'Like a woman with appendicitis,' she said, 'but I've seen hundreds of them in my last rotation and she's not quite fitting the mould. I want to scan her, but her LMP was only nine or so weeks ago, and it might need a transvaginal scan to pick up anything.'

He nodded abruptly. 'OK. Let's have a look at her and make sure. Don't want to miss anything.'

So yet again Jenny was prodded, and they scanned her. And, sure enough, she had a tubal pregnancy that was on the point of rupture.

'Jenny, I'm afraid you've got a problem,' he said gently. 'The egg's implanted in the wrong place, and it's trying to grow inside your Fallopian tube. I'm sorry, there's nothing we can do except remove it before it ruptures the tube and causes severe haemorrhaging.'

She stared at him, her eyes filling. 'Are you sure? Isn't there any way it can stay there?

He shook his head. 'No. I'm really very sorry, but I'm afraid your pregnancy isn't viable. The tube simply isn't big enough to contain the developing foetus, and at some point in the near future it will rupture, and the foetus will die. If we don't act, it could kill you, too.'

'No. I don't believe you. I wouldn't die—that's a wild exaggeration!'

Eve held her breath, watching him closely for any subtle hint of grief, but there was none. Just a firming of his lips. 'Unfortunately not,' he said evenly. 'Ectopic pregnancy is the commonest cause of maternal mortality in the first trimester. I'm really sorry, Jenny, but there's nothing we can do. Your symptoms indicate that your Fallopian tube is beginning to rupture. You need an emergency operation to remove it, and it's much better to do it now in a controlled way than later in a tearing hurry because you're bleeding severely.'

Jenny closed her eyes and a tear trickled down her cheek. 'I didn't even know I was pregnant,' she whispered. 'I need to call my husband.'

'By all means. We'll get you moved up to the ward and prep you for Theatre, and then take you down as soon as possible. When did you last eat?'

She shrugged. 'I don't know. Last night? Yesterday, anyway. I've been feeling too rough all day today to eat.'

'OK. We'll get you into Theatre as soon as we can.'

They left her and walked back to the ward. Eve wondered if he'd say anything, but he just gave her a strained smile and said, 'Well done. Want to do the op?'

She didn't, not really, because although it was inevitable, it was effectively a termination and she hadn't done one yet, but this was at least utterly unavoidable and she had to start somewhere.

'OK,' she said, and he smiled again encouragingly.

'I'll see you up there with her in a while, then,' he said, and disappeared into the theatre lift, leaving her to carry on alone to the ward.

She managed the operation on Jenny, removing the swollen, distended tube with the beginnings of a tear and suturing the small incision without a hitch. Through it all Hugh was silent, but as she straightened up he said, 'Well done. Thank you. Right, next I need you to do a section. It's utterly straightforward, a breech presentation in a first baby, with a planned delivery date and no adverse indications except that the placenta's right across the front of the uterus.'

She felt her eyes widen. 'Oh, cheers! Where will you be?'

'Assisting you, silly,' he said with a smile touching his eyes over the mask. 'I wasn't going to abandon you completely. But she'll be conscious, so I won't be telling you what to do. Just remember to ask if you need to.'

She didn't. It was, as he'd said, a textbook case, and he'd gone through it with her in the break while Theatre was being prepped for the next case, so she felt well prepared. And although it was technically more challenging, the satisfaction was huge, and she felt the still-new thrill of being the first person to touch the baby as she reached in and eased it out through the incision.

'It's a girl,' she said, her voice choked, holding the baby up so the parents could see her. She knew her eyes would be bright with tears, as ever, but no one seemed to mind. 'Congratulations.'

'Oh, she's beautiful,' the mother whispered, starting to cry, and Eve had to blink hard to clear her own vision before she could complete the delivery.

Hugh had clamped the cord and sucked out the baby's nose and mouth, and he handed her, still wet and bloody and screaming, to her mother. The screams settled to a drizzling hiccup, and then stopped, calmed by the mother's tender murmurings. Eve had to shut her ears and cut herself off from all that maternal bliss, reminding herself that she had a job to do.

'Well done,' Hugh murmured as she finished closing, and his eyes over the mask were warm with approval. He tugged it down and turned to the patient with a smile. 'Right, let's get you back to the ward and you can settle down with a cup of tea and feed the baby. Any names yet?'

'I don't know.' The mother, Liz, looked at Eve over the top of the drapes. 'What's your name?'

'Eve,' she replied, and Liz smiled.

'Eve. I like that. Can we call her Eve?' she asked her husband, and he nodded, smiling thoughtfully.

'Eve—yes. It's lovely. If you don't mind?'

'Of course I don't mind,' Eve said, feeling herself tearing up again. Heavens, this was starting to be a habit!

'Told you,' Hugh murmured as they left the theatre. 'It's a good job you aren't called Ermintrude.'

'It's a good job I'm not called Ermintrude anyway,' she retorted. 'My parents have got enough to answer for as it is.'

He shot her a curious look, but she changed the subject quickly, quizzing him on her performance. 'So, come on, what did I do wrong?'

'Nothing.'

'I must have done something. Too small or too large an incision? Too far round? Too high? Too low?'

'No.'

'Too slow? Pulled the baby out wrong?'

He shook his head, a slow, lazy smile spreading over his face. 'Nothing. You can't get out of it. It was perfect. If she'd been my wife, I would have been happy for you to deliver her.'

Wow. That was a compliment and a half, she thought, and felt the glow all the way to her toes.

'So, what next?'

He laughed. 'You can do the rest of the list, if you like. I'll just hold the retractors and doze quietly in the corner.'

'Don't you dare doze,' she warned, feeling a touch of panic. What if she did something wrong?

'Stop worrying. You'll be fine, and of course I won't doze.' He gave her a thoughtful look. 'You've got no confidence, have you? Lots of guts, and plenty of bravado, but no real confidence. It's all show, and I think most of it's put on for your own benefit, to convince yourself that you really can do it. Am I right?'

Too right, and too close to the knuckle. 'I just want to be sure,' she said lightly, but she couldn't meet his eyes again and stalled by fiddling with the drawstring on her trousers.

He wasn't having any, though, and, putting a finger under her chin, he tilted her head up to his. 'You're good,' he told her seriously. 'You spotted the ectopic when it was presenting like an appendix, and that takes skill. Believe it. Believe in yourself.'

She swallowed, wanting to cry again, but there wasn't time. 'Our next patient will be here,' she said, and headed for the sink to scrub. With a sigh Hugh followed her, saying nothing more for the rest of the day except to praise, encourage and inform when necessary.

That evening he left her in charge of emergencies, and it was predictably busy. She coped, though, and didn't need to call him in—mainly because nothing that drastic happened—but his words earlier about her self-confidence made her more determined than ever to cope alone.

And she did, to her relief. At three in the morning, she shot downstairs to the canteen while the going was good, and grabbed a quick meal. While she was there she checked her phone, which was on silent, and realised she'd missed her alarm call reminder to take her pill.

'Idiot,' she muttered, fumbling for it in her bag, and taking it immediately. Nine hours late, and it wasn't the first time, but even though she had to take it promptly because it was a progestogen-only pill, she should still be safe. She'd been told twelve hours, max, because this was a stronger one than some of the single-hormone pills which had to be taken extremely regularly. But it was just as well she'd opted for this one because of her hectic schedule, knowing it would be more likely to be safe if she was held up and took it late.

It had to be. She wasn't going to risk ending up in here having a termination, like some of their patients, although she didn't think, if the crunch came, she could bring herself to do it. And she couldn't take time off to have a baby, so she'd just have to make sure she didn't get pregnant.

Not that she'd be able to tell. Her system had been utterly confused by the introduction of the hormones, and she hadn't had a period since she'd started taking the Pill weeks before.

All the more reason to be careful, she told herself, and vowed to be more punctual with her pill-taking.

Her bleep went, and she gulped down the rest of her coffee, grabbed the last bite of her sandwich and headed back to Maternity.

'OK if I leave you?'

'Fine,' she said with a smile. She'd finished the operation, was just closing, and Hugh knew he could let her get on with it. The last few weeks had seen her ability and her confidence grow in leaps and bounds, and she was beginning to fulfill her great potential. She was going to be a fantastic surgeon, tackling everything she did with her trade-mark enthusiasm and dedication.

And that was just at work. At home, with him and his children, she was rapidly becoming an essential part of his life, although she stonewalled him every time he tried to bring up the subject of their relationship. Despite that, he knew that Eve was more and more comfortable with it and beginning to feel like part of the family.

So long as he didn't try and talk about it, or tell her that he loved her.

Not that he had, not yet, because he'd sensed from the beginning that it would make her uncomfortable, and he didn't want to frighten her off, but now he was finding it harder and harder. So many times a day he wanted to put his arms round her and hug her and tell her he loved her, like he did with the kids, like he had with Jo.

He'd never thought he'd love like that again, and it scared him a little, but he wasn't running away from it, and he wasn't going to let Eve run away from it any longer either.

It was just working out how to tell her.

He headed to his office, intent on doing paperwork, and Maggie dutifully lined up a veritable rainforest requiring his attention.

'This much?' he said wretchedly, and she laughed.

'You've been avoiding it,' she pointed out, and he knew it was true. He'd spent too long with Eve, stolen time away from his responsibilities. With a sigh he settled down to work his way through it.

'Coffee would be good,' he murmured, and a cup appeared at his side in seconds. 'Maggie, you're a star.'

'I know. Keep working.'

'Yes, Mummy.'

She slapped his hand and disappeared into her own office next door, leaving him chuckling. He was lucky to have her.

* * *

She'd just done a quick ward round, checking on her post-ops, when Eve felt the first cramping pain. She rubbed her back absently. Too much time crouched on the stool doing gynae ops, she thought, but the next stab was lower and seemed deeper inside her, more abdominal.

And then the next.

The pains were coming in waves, she realised, evenly spaced. Like contractions.

No. She must have a tummy bug, she thought, but they felt like period pains, and her heart sank. She'd only had a few odd days of bleeding here and there since she'd gone on the Pill. Obviously her body had decided that it was time for a full-on dysmenorrhoeic horror show, and it had chosen to today to start.

Fabulous. They still had a clinic this afternoon, and she really didn't need—

'Ahhh!'

'Eve?'

She looked up, her mouth open, gasping with the pain, and found Sam frowning down at her in concern.

'I'm fine,' she said, trying to smile. 'It's just a period pain. I'll be all right.'

'Funny period pain,' he said quietly. 'Do you usually get them?'

She shook her head, then felt a strange flooding sensation and glanced down, sucking in her breath at the spreading red stain on her pale blue theatre scrubs.

'Right. In here,' Sam said firmly, wheeling her through a door into an empty side ward that had just been vacated. 'Lie down.'

'Sam, I'm fine.'

'Let me be the judge of that,' he said, his warm, gentle hands exploring her abdomen thoroughly. 'When was your last period?'

She shrugged. 'I don't know. I haven't had a proper one since I went on the Pill.'

'Which was when?'

'The middle of April,' she said. It was now the middle of July, and she truly had no idea when her last period before then had been. Two weeks? Three? 'That must be why this one's so bad.'

Sam grunted noncommittally and straightened up. 'Let's get some obs on you and find out what's going on. When did you last pee?'

'I have no idea.'

'Good. I'll do an ultrasound. Stay there.'

He popped out, but he was only gone a moment, returning with a nurse, a portable obs unit and an ultrasound machine. 'This isn't as good as the one downstairs, but it'll tell me what I want to know.'

She didn't ask. She didn't want to know what he was looking for. She knew, anyway, but she said nothing, just lay there and let them all rush around her, obliging them with a urine sample, and then listening in a kind of shocked limbo to Sam's gently delivered verdict.

'You've almost certainly had a miscarriage,' he told her, sitting beside her and wrapping her hand in his. 'A better ultrasound will confirm it, and we'll take you down for one shortly. Your pregnancy test was positive, but it would be for some days after the death of a foetus, and I wouldn't want you to hold out any false hope. I don't know yet if your uterus is going to empty itself spontaneously or if we'll need to take you to Theatre to do a D and C, but your blood pressure's stable and your pulse is nice and steady, so I don't think anything untoward is about to happen. I take it you didn't realise you were pregnant?'

She shook her head numbly. 'I had no idea.'

He nodded. 'How's the pain?'

'Receding a bit.' Her fingers tightened on his and she met his eyes pleadingly. 'Sam—don't tell Hugh.'

'I take it this is his baby?'

She nodded, her heart aching. 'Of course it is, and he'll be devastated, but I just need time to think—to get used to the idea, before I see him.'

'OK. I'll try and stall him as long as possible.'

But it wasn't possible.

Sam left the room, closing the door quietly behind him, and ran straight into Hugh at the first corner.

'What the hell's going on? Someone said Eve's had a miscarriage. Where is she?'

'My office, now,' he said, and steered his friend away from the ward, sitting him down and telling him, as gently as he could, what had happened.

Hugh was stunned. He stared at Sam, stared at his hands, scrubbed a hand round the back of his neck and stood up, pacing the floor for a moment before looking at Sam again, unable to believe what his friend had just told him. It couldn't be…

'How the hell did she get pregnant? When? She's on the Pill.'

'She doesn't know. She had no idea she was pregnant. She asked me not to tell you, and I wasn't going to if you hadn't already heard, to give her time to think about it, let it sink in for a while before she spoke to you. I think you should give her some time.'

Time to get her defences in order, he realised, but he wasn't having it. This was his baby, too, and if they were losing it, they were doing it together.

'Tough,' he said, ripping open the door. 'I need to be with her—and, before you say it, she needs to be with me. Can you get cover for us?'

'Sure.' Sam's hand curled over his shoulder and squeezed. 'For what it's worth, I'm really sorry, Hugh.'

He wrapped his fingers over Sam's hand and squeezed back, swallowing the lump in his throat. 'Thanks. And thanks for looking after her.'

He headed back to the ward, tapping lightly on her door before pushing it open and going in. She was lying with her eyes closed, her head turned away, but he could see the tears on her cheeks and he knew she wasn't asleep.

'Eve?' he murmured.

She took a shaky breath. 'I didn't know,' she said emptily. 'I had our baby inside me and I didn't know, and now it's dead, and I didn't even know I was having it.'

He felt his eyes glaze with tears, and sitting on the bed he gathered her into his arms and rocked her as she wept.

'Oh, darling, I'm so sorry,' he whispered.

'Sam wants to scan me later,' she said unsteadily. 'To see if there's anything left.' Her voice broke, and he wrapped her closer against his chest and shushed her.

'Oh, sweetheart…'

There was nothing he could say, nothing that would take away the awful realisation that her child—their child—had died. So he just held her, lying on the bed beside her and cradling her in his arms, not caring when the nurses who knew him so well came in to check her obs from time to time.

After a while she slept, the boneless, exhausted sleep of someone in shock, and he found his own eyes closing. If only he could stay there with her, but he had the kids to see to, and patients needing his attention— No. Sam had sorted that out. Just the kids, then, and they didn't really need him.

He needed them, though, needed to know that two of his children were still alive. He shifted slightly, and Eve opened her eyes and looked up at him, puzzled for a moment before her memory returned and her eyes dropped shut again and the tears slid out from under her lids.

'I didn't even know,' she said sadly. 'That's the worst bit. It seems so unkind that I had a child and I didn't even know it was there, or acknowledge it. I never had time to love it, Hugh.' He felt her stiffen, felt the thoughts tumbling in her head, and she struggled up into a sitting position. 'Hugh, what if I did something wrong? What if the baby died because of something I did, because I was too stupid to realise I was pregnant?'

'No!' No, he couldn't let her think that. He shook his head, reaching out to her. 'You've done nothing wrong, Eve. You've had the occasional glass of wine, you eat a very sensible diet, you haven't been exposed to X-rays or chemicals—there's nothing to blame yourself for. It's just one of those things that happens.'

'I was still taking the Pill.'

'That won't have harmed it.'

She sighed and scrubbed her hand over her nose. 'Do you suppose there was something wrong with it?'

He shrugged and sat up, shifting so she was back in his arms, propped against the pillows, cradled firmly against his heart where she belonged, if she only had the sense to realise it. 'Probably. There is in a high proportion of miscarriages.'

'Poor baby,' she said, her eyes filling again, and she turned into his chest and hugged him tight. 'Thank you for being here for me,' she mumbled into his shirt, and he smoothed her hair and hugged her back.

'Of course I'm here for you. I'm always here for you. I always will be. I love you, Eve. Where else would I be?'

She tipped back her head and looked at him blankly for a moment, then turned away, moving out of his arms. 'No. No, Hugh, you don't. This is just a knee-jerk reaction.'

He shook his head and sighed. 'No, it isn't, Eve. You know I love you. I've loved you for months. And I don't know why you're aren't comfortable with it, and I know this isn't the time to talk about it, but I can't pretend it doesn't matter any more, that you don't matter, because you do. And we can get through this.'

'I can get through it,' she said. 'I've got through worse things.' She looked at her watch. 'Don't you need to be getting home for the kids?'

'They'll keep.'

'No. Please, Hugh, I want to be alone for a while. I need time to think. Go home to your family. I'll be fine. Sam's taking good care of me.'

And because she seemed so adamant, because there was nothing he could say to change her mind, he went home, and sat his kids down in the kitchen, and told them.

'Eve's had a miscarriage,' he said, and to his horror he heard his voice crack, and tears filled his eyes, and then Lucy's arms were round him, and Tom was holding his hand, and, safe in the heart of his loving and supportive little family, he wept for the child he'd lost and the woman who didn't want to love him.

CHAPTER TEN

'SAM, can you do me a favour?'

Sam studied Eve thoughtfully, perched on the end of the bed and nodded. 'I'll try.'

'Can you get me down for this scan when Hugh's not around? I really don't want him there.'

Sam sighed, studying his hands for a second before meeting her eyes. 'He loves you, you know.'

'I know. I still don't want him there. Please.'

'OK. I'll do what I can. He's got no right of access to your notes anyway, but that won't stop him looking at them if they're in with the others.'

'So don't leave them in with the others. Put them somewhere else.'

He sighed again, nodded briefly and stood up. 'OK. He'll probably kick up a fuss, but I can deal with him. I'll wait till he's gone.'

She felt the pressure ease a little. Stupid, really, because the scan was just routine, to prove that the pregnancy had ended and to make sure her uterus was empty and she didn't need surgery. It wouldn't matter if Hugh was there or not, but for some reason she wanted this small private moment to say goodbye to her child.

The child she hadn't wanted, had no time for at this stage in her life, who would have skewed all her plans and trashed her carefully orchestrated career path. The child who, in the last few hours, had stolen a corner of his mother's heart for ever.

Sam was true to his word. She went down for the ultrasound at ten past seven, with Hugh safely at home and utterly unaware. Sam went with her, watching the screen as Mike, the radiologist, smeared gel on her smooth, flat abdomen—an abdomen doomed to remain flat for the foreseeable future—and searched for the evidence of her miscarriage.

Mike grunted, leant closer, moved the probe a little, stared at the screen again, then frowned. 'That's interesting.'

'What?' she asked, turning her head to look at the screen.

'Looks like another foetus,' he said. He used a blunt finger to point to a tiny little curve on the edge of her uterus. 'Here—and here, this is the remains of a pregnancy. That must be the one you lost.' He pointed to another little area, no more than a blip. Then he went back to the first little area, the curve, and zoomed in closer—close enough to see a tiny, tiny flutter in the centre of the curve.

'See that?' he said, pointing at it and smiling at her sympathetically. 'That's a heartbeat—only the one, I'm sorry to say. The other one's definitely gone. There's just a little shred of membrane left, and that'll soon be discharged, I think. It's not attached at all. You must have been pregnant with twins.'

'Gestation?' Sam asked, while Eve lay there and stared in stunned silence at the tiny flutter that was her baby's beating heart.

'About eight weeks? Give or take.'

'Can I see it again?' she asked, still reeling with shock, and the radiologist moved the probe back.

'There. Want a photo?'

She gulped and shook her head. 'No.'

Because it was unnecessary. The image was engraved on her heart for ever. She would need no other reminders of this child she was almost bound to lose. There had been too much pain, too much blood for it to remain secure.

Mike, however, seemed to have a different opinion. 'It looks fine. I would say there must have been something wrong with the other twin rather than with the pregnancy, and there's certainly no uterine abnormality,' he was saying to them, and Sam was nodding thoughtfully, but all Eve could think of was what would happen next.

'I'm likely to lose it, though, aren't I?' she asked, and they both looked at her, Sam a little more keenly.

'Can't say,' Mike told her. 'There's nothing showing on this scan to indicate that you will, but time will tell. Sorry, can't be more specific. The 3D scanner might pick up more. We can have a look in the morning with that, if you like.'

'We'll discuss it tomorrow,' Sam said. He wheeled her back up to the ward, closed the door of her little side room and stood for a long moment looking down at her in silence.

'Did you know it was twins?' she asked him eventually, and he shook his head.

'Not for sure. I had a feeling you were still pregnant, but it was too small to see clearly enough on the portable machine and there was too much blood for it to be that baby. That rather hinted at twins, and it's not uncommon. And the HCG was a little high in your pregnancy test. That rather indicated another foetus. We'll get a good view tomorrow with the 3D scanner. It might give us a better idea of all sorts of things.'

She reached out and caught his hand, the realisation of what was facing her just starting to hit home. 'Sam, please don't tell Hugh,' she said, panicking. 'I really don't want him to know about this. Let's just tell him I've lost the baby and leave it at that. It's not a lie. Buy me time.'

Sam frowned. 'Eve, it's his child. He ought to know. And he loves you.'

She looked away, feeling the pain starting to build like pressure behind her breastbone. 'I know, but I need time to think, to get used to it. Please?'

He nodded reluctantly. 'OK. I'll see you in the morning and we'll get the other scan. Try and sleep tonight.' He squeezed her hand and released it, then left her alone with her tumbling emotions. Sleep? Not a chance.

She was still pregnant. Pregnant and, unless nature took its course, facing the most monumental decision of her life.

'What do you mean, I can't look?'

Sam sighed wearily. 'Hugh, she's not your patient. You don't have access to her notes.'

'That's ridiculous!'

'No, it's her right, and I'm going to respect it. I'm sorry. She'll tell you if there's anything she wants you to know.'

'And you won't? Dammit, I thought you were my friend.'

Sam sighed and scrubbed a hand through his hair. 'Hugh, don't make this any harder for me.'

'And what about me? What about how hard it is for me?'

'This isn't about you, it's about her,' he said firmly.

'She's lost a baby, and she's feeling very vulnerable at the moment, and you need to respect that.'

Hugh swallowed hard, feeling a ridiculous stab of pain at Sam's confirmation that their baby had died. He'd known anyway, really, but while the pregnancy test had still shown positive, there had been a shred of hope.

Now that hope was gone, and he nodded acceptance, patted Sam awkwardly on the arm and apologised for giving him such a hard time. He went up to the ward to see Eve, and was told she was resting, so he went back to his clinic and growled at Maggie and Oliver and tried to concentrate.

On the way back to the ward at the end of his clinic, he bumped into Julia. The last person he wanted to see, but she put a hand on his arm and said softly, 'I'm so sorry, Hugh. You don't deserve this, either of you. She's a lovely girl, you were right. Is she OK?'

He stared at her in amazement. 'Um—yes, I think so. I'm just going back up there.'

'Give her my love.'

But he didn't, because when he reached the ward, he found she'd been discharged and gone home. 'How could you let her go home alone?' he raved at Sam, but Sam simply sighed and let him get it out of his system.

'She's fine, Hugh. She's gone home to rest, and if you've got any sense you'll let her. Right now what she needs to do is sleep and heal.'

He was right, of course, but it didn't make it any easier when all he wanted to do was gather her into his arms and hold her. He tried to concentrate, tried to work, but he'd grown so used to having her by his side that it seemed odd without her.

He couldn't get her out of his mind—and when, later, he went to see Sam about a patient and found not Sam but Eve's notes on his desk, there was no way he wasn't going to scan through them.

And when he did, the shock of what he read took the legs out from under him.

'Hugh, what the hell are you doing?'

He raised his head and met Sam's furious eyes steadily.

'Reading her notes,' he said, with what he felt was commendable calm, under the circumstances.

Sam snatched the notes from him and slammed them shut, hurling them in a drawer and locking it. Hugh inclined his head towards it.

'That'll be handy when she's brought in in the night because she's lost the other twin.'

Sam swore viciously. 'You weren't supposed to know.'

'She's pregnant with my child and *I wasn't supposed to know*?' he roared, getting to his feet. 'Dammit, Sam, why didn't you *tell* me?'

'Because she asked me not to.'

'Why? Why wouldn't she want me to know? Unless…' He stared at Sam in horror, the truth dawning. 'Oh, my God. She's going to get rid of it. She's going to have a termination, isn't she? *Isn't she?'*

Sam shook his head wordlessly. 'Hugh, you're jumping to conclusions. I can't discuss this with you, you know that.'

'No, but I can discuss it with her,' he said. Thrusting Sam out of the way, he went into his office and found Maggie.

'Field my calls,' he said crisply. 'And page Oliver and tell him he's in charge. I'm out of the hospital for a while.'

'But—'

He didn't give her time for any buts, just grabbed his jacket and keys, and left. His phone was in his pocket, but he had no intention of phoning her. He'd just go round there, confront her, make her talk about it, because this was ridiculous and there was no way she was going through with something so monumental without discussing it with him first.

And she didn't even need to let him in. She'd had a spare set of keys cut for her flat weeks ago, after she'd been shut out, and she'd given them to him to hang on to for her. They were still in the glovebox of his car, and he was going to use them now for the first time. They could talk about the ethics of it later.

Eve slipped off her clothes, crawled into the middle of her bed and curled into a ball. She was so tired, so tired and sad and confused, weighed down by the impossibility of her position and crushed by a wave of grief so huge she couldn't even comprehend it.

This time yesterday she hadn't even been aware that she was pregnant. Now her whole life had been thrown into turmoil, and nothing would ever be the same again.

She didn't cry. Some things, she'd heard, went too deep to cry for, and this, it seemed, was one of them.

Instead she lay there, not even really thinking, just allowing the pain to wash over her, until finally she slept.

The sound of a key in her door woke her three hours later. Puzzled, she sat up, wondering if she'd imagined it, but she hadn't. Hugh stood there in her bedroom doorway, his eyes tortured, and she thought, He knows. He knows about the twin. Her heart, already over-burdened, sank still further.

'How did you get in?'

He held the keys up, dangling them in front of her. 'I think it's time we had a chat, don't you?'

She scooted up the bed, hunching over, hugging her knees. He looked—no, not angry, but hurt, confused, puzzled. A lump lodged itself in her throat and she looked away, unable to meet those sad, accusing eyes. 'You could have phoned—rung the doorbell. Anything.'

'And given you a chance to put the chain on the door and deadlock it? I don't think so, not this time, Eve. I'm going to put the kettle on, and I'm going to make you something to eat and drink, and you're going to talk to me, whether you like it or not.'

She didn't. She really, really didn't, but she guessed he was going nowhere, so when the door clicked shut she got up, feeling oddly light-headed, pulled on a dressing-gown and went through into the living room.

'Tea or coffee?'

Eve shook her head. 'Not tea. I really don't fancy it at the moment. I'll have fruit juice—there's some in the fridge.'

He set it down in front of her on the coffee-table, his eyes concerned, but she couldn't meet them and looked away, and he went back into the kitchen and started to fix himself a coffee.

'Why didn't you tell me you were still pregnant?' he asked softly, and she swallowed and fiddled with the belt of her dressing-gown.

'I wasn't sure I was,' she lied, and she heard his hand slam down on the kitchen worktop.

'Of course you knew. You knew last night—that's why you wouldn't see me today. Eve, I've looked at your notes.'

Her head yanked up at that, and she met his eyes then, furious. 'You had no right—'

'Let's not talk about rights,' he said, every bit as furious. 'There's a baby's rights here that are more important than yours or mine, and they're the only ones I'm interested in.'

Her eyes filled with tears, and she looked away hastily, but not fast enough, apparently, because he sighed and came and sat down opposite her on the coffee-table, pushing the fruit juice out of the way and taking her hands.

'Oh, hell, Eve, I'm sorry.'

She shook her head and clung to him, needing him even though she couldn't bear to face him.

'I love you, Eve,' he said raggedly. 'Don't shut me out.'

'I have to,' she said, the tears filling her eyes now not for her or for her babies, but for Hugh, their father, the man she loved more than she would ever have believed possible.

'Oh, sweetheart,' he said gently, and wrapped her in his arms, shifting so he was on the sofa and she was on his lap, cradled against his heart with her head on his shoulder and her arms locked tightly around him. 'You don't have to shut me out. You can talk to me. Surely there's something I can do?'

She gave a shaky laugh. If only. There was nothing anyone could do. She'd made a promise and she'd failed, because she hadn't even been organised enough to take her pills on time.

Oh, Daddy, she thought sadly, her father's stern face clear in her mind. Why can't I get it right even now, so many, many years later? Why must I always disappoint you?

'There's nothing you can do. There's nothing to talk

about. I promised my father I'd do this, and I have to do it—somehow.'

He stared at her in confusion. 'Do what? What did you promise him that's more important than this?'

She struggled off his lap, picked up her juice and went out onto the balcony. The last rays of the evening sun were just coming over the trees opposite, and she sat down at her little table and stared sightlessly at the river.

'Eve? Talk to me.'

She had to. They couldn't, after all, sit in silence indefinitely, so she talked about the only thing that she could deal with at the moment, because she'd been dealing with it for years and another night wasn't going to hurt her.

'My father was a tyrant,' she told him quietly. 'No, that's unfair. He was a surgeon, and he was talented, skilful and he set exacting standards, for himself and for everybody else. I never lived up to them. No matter how hard I tried, I never managed to be good enough for him. I was a girl, and he wanted a son to follow in his footsteps, but my brother was a waste of space. I tried to make up for his shortcomings, but I couldn't do it.'

'So that's what this is all about? Being good enough for your father?' He sighed and sat down on the other chair, crossing one ankle over the other knee and staring out across the water. 'Eve, I'm a father. There's no way I'd want my daughter to do anything that made her this unhappy.'

'But I'm not unhappy. I love medicine—'

'I'm talking about the baby.'

She gasped, sucking in air, clamping down the sob, willing him to stop, but he didn't.

'Just tell me something. If you hadn't made your father

that promise, if you'd just found yourself in this situation, with me, with the baby—would you still want to have a termination?'

She stared at him in horror, tears spilling unchecked from her eyes. 'I don't want to have a termination!'

'So marry me.'

She sucked in a huge breath and shook her head. 'No! No, Hugh, I can't!'

'Because of some stupid bloody promise?'

He closed his eyes, scrubbing his hands over his face, hauling in a steadying breath before he opened his eyes and looked at her again.

She was killing him. She could see that, see the pain in his eyes, the drawn lines bracketing his mouth. And she knew just how much he was hurting, because it was tearing her apart inside.

'I can't let him down, Hugh,' she said.

'And this doesn't change anything? The fact that you're pregnant with his grandchild? What about letting your baby down? What about letting me down? Eve, he was your father. He loved you—'

'Did he? He never said so.'

His face was stunned. 'What? I tell my kids every day—more than that. Every time I talk to them. They've never been in any doubt.'

'I know.' She felt the sobs welling. Her child could have that. Could have Hugh as a father, could know the warmth and emotional security of his love, if only…

'Eve, please,' he said. 'Think about it carefully. You don't have to give up work. You don't have to change your career plan. I've brought up two children alone and I was a consultant at thirty-two. You can do it, if it's really so important to you.'

'It is! It's who I am, Hugh. I love being a doctor, but my baby—my baby…'

She started to cry again, huge racking sobs, and with a muttered curse Hugh scooped her up and carried her back inside her apartment where they'd have more privacy, kicking the door shut and sitting with her, rocking her against his chest while she cried and cried and cried.

'Why couldn't he love me?' she sobbed. 'Why couldn't he be proud of me? Why couldn't he be like you are with your kids? Why did he have to hate me?'

'I don't believe he hated you. Maybe he just couldn't talk about his feelings. Lots of people can't. And maybe he was just too unwell. How long was he ill?'

She sniffed and found a tissue in her hand, and scrubbed at her nose. 'Um—years, really. He had a bad heart. And Andrew didn't help. He was a bit of a wild child—he wasn't as bad as he led them to believe, or he would be dead by now, but he got into a bad crowd, and—he was awful. And Dad couldn't deal with it. I spent years mediating, keeping the peace, stopping them all from killing each other. I went to bed every night with screaming ringing in my ears, and it didn't matter what I did, I couldn't change it. All I wanted was for him to tell me that he loved me, and for my mother to be happy, but she was stuck at home with us, and she hated it. I can't imagine anything worse than being trapped like she was, expected to run the home and deal with all the flak—'

'That's what this is all about, isn't it?' he cut in, his voice quietly incredulous. 'It's nothing to do with a deathbed promise, and if it is, it shouldn't be. You're a good doctor, an excellent doctor, and if your father wasn't proud of you, then he didn't deserve you. But I do, Eve. I love you. I'm proud of you, and you won't have me. Why? Are you afraid to marry me because you don't want to live with my kids?'

She shrugged helplessly, not sure any longer what she did feel. So much—too much to tell one fear from another. She felt the panic rising and struggled out of his lap, walking to the window, wrapping her arms around her waist to hold herself together. 'I don't know. I couldn't bear to end up like my mother, trapped in the house with a teenage monster—'

'But my kids aren't monsters, Eve. You like them, and they love you. I love you. And I wouldn't expect you to stay at home and look after my children. They don't need that. They haven't had a mother for eleven years. Why would they need one now?'

She turned, and found him right behind her, his eyes warm and sincere and loving. Did she dare to believe him? 'You'd allow me to carry on working?' she said cautiously.

'Allow?' He gave a strained little laugh. 'Of course I'd *allow* you to carry on working—unless you decided not to. But it would be your choice. Everything about your career would be your choice. Even if you wanted to go away and continue your training in another hospital, we'd get round it.'

'And—the baby?'

'We'll deal with it. We'll set up some child-care arrangements that fit in with whatever suits us. We could have a nanny—the house is big enough—or we could move. Whatever. The baby won't suffer. We'll make sure of it, and my kids love you. We could make it work, Eve. We could.'

She sucked in a huge breath.

'You make it sound so easy.'

He shook his head, his laugh this time a little rueful. 'Oh, no, Eve, it won't be easy, but we'll manage, because we love each other, and we'll love the baby, and we'll cope, because as long as we have each other, that's all that matters.'

'And you wouldn't feel trapped? You were trapped before, when Jo got pregnant—'

He shook his head emphatically. 'No. No, I wasn't trapped. I loved Jo desperately. We needed to be together. We were two halves of a whole, and I was lost without her. I never thought I'd love like that again, but I was wrong. I do, and being with you could never be a trap, Eve. Never.'

She stared at him for ages, unable to believe what he was saying, reading his eyes until finally, at last, she was able to trust what she could see there.

Her hand slid down over her baby, and tears welled up and spilled down her cheeks. 'I was never going to have a termination,' she said softly. 'I didn't know what I was going to do, but that was never on the cards.'

'But—I thought…'

She shook her head and smiled. 'No, you assumed. You were afraid for the baby, and you assumed that was what I was going to do. I couldn't have done it. I didn't know what I was going to do, but that didn't even enter my head.'

'But—Sam said…' He trailed off, stabbed his fingers through his hair and laughed a little wildly. 'No. Sam said I was jumping to conclusions. I just assumed—you're right. And for the record, I was afraid for you as well as the baby. I thought it would destroy you.'

She nodded sadly. 'It would, which is why it was never an option. But I didn't know what on earth I was going to do.'

'And now?'

She summoned a smile, albeit a wobbly one. 'Now, if you really meant it, I'll marry you. I love your kids, too, and I know they're good kids. I was just panicking, afraid of being trapped like my mother, and I hadn't even realised that was at the bottom of it. I was just running, but not any more. I love you, Hugh. I can't imagine life without you—if you'll have me.'

And her smile became all wobbly, and the tears cascaded down her cheeks, and with a choked laugh he pulled her into his arms and cradled her against his chest and kissed away the tears, his lips finding hers and clinging to them as if he'd never let her go.

That was good. She didn't want him to, ever, and she went up on tiptoe, threaded her fingers through his hair and kissed him back as if she'd die without him.

After an age he lifted his head and tucked her beneath his chin, with the steady beat of his heart beneath her ear and his lips pressed against her temple. It felt so wonderful—so incredibly right. 'I love you,' she whispered. 'Marry me really soon?'

He laughed, a broken, ragged sound, quickly stifled. 'Of course I'll marry you soon, you silly girl,' he murmured unevenly. 'Just try and stop me.'

'No,' she said, snuggling closer. 'No, I won't stop you. I love you much too much.'

'I'm so proud of you, Eve,' he said softly. 'You're a fantastic doctor, and you're a beautiful woman, and you'll be a wonderful mother. I love you.'

Proud of her. At last, someone she loved was proud of her. She lifted her head to Hugh, exhausted with emotion but with something still left to do. 'We need to tell your children.'

His arm tightened around her. 'Of course. Are you sure you're up to it?'

She nodded. 'I'd like to tell them with you.'

Hugh looked at her, and she glanced down at herself and gave a rueful smile. 'I suppose I ought to get dressed.'

Hugh smiled back. 'Probably.'

'Tom? Lucy? Can you come down?'

They thundered down the stairs, stopping dead in the hall and staring at Eve in surprise.

'Hi. I thought you were in hospital?' Tom said, puzzled.

'They let me out earlier. I'm all right now.'

'I'm really sorry about the baby,' Lucy said, running to her and hugging her gently. Eve stood there for a second, then her arms came round the girl and hugged her back, tears filling her eyes.

'Thank you,' she whispered, deeply touched by Lucy's genuine affection.

'Um—yeah,' Tom said, looking uncomfortable. 'Hope you're OK now. It must have been rough.'

She smiled at him. 'It was, and I'm still sad, but there's something else…'

'It was a twin,' Hugh said, taking over when she ran out of words. 'She's still pregnant. There's another baby.'

Lucy looked up at her and her eyes widened with delight. 'You're still having a baby? Amazing! I'm going to have a baby sister or brother—oh, that's so cool!'

'And we're getting married,' Hugh added, wrapping an

arm around Eve from the other side and reaching out for Tom. 'I hope you guys are OK with that?'

'OK? It's wonderful—and about time,' his son said gruffly, a suspicious brightness in his eyes. He moved into his father's embrace and reached for Lucy, his arm lying over Eve's, closing the circle of love.

0706/108/MB039

The child she loves…is his child.

And now he knows…

THE SEVEN YEAR SECRET BY ROZ DENNY FOX

Mallory Forester's daughter needs a transplant. But there's only one person left to turn to – Liddy's father. Mallory hasn't seen Connor in seven years, and now she has to tell him he's a father…with a chance to save his daughter's life!

HIS DADDY'S EYES BY DEBRA SALONEN

Judge Lawrence Bishop spent a weekend in the arms of a sexy stranger two years ago and he's been looking for her ever since. He discovers she's dead, but *her baby son* is living with his aunt, Sara Carsten. Ren does the maths and realises he's got to see pretty Sara, talk to her and go from there…

Look for more *Little Secrets* coming in August!

On sale 7th July 2006

www.millsandboon.co.uk

M&B™

0606/108/MB038

Escape to...

19th May 2006

16th June 2006

21st July 2006

18th August 2006

Available at WH Smith, Tesco, ASDA, Borders, Eason, Sainsbury's and all good paperback bookshops

www.millsandboon.co.uk